This is it, Tessa. Time to make a move.

Noah's eyes lit with a heat that she felt burning inside her, too. He lifted one hand and smoothed a strand of her hair back from her face and the tips of his fingers slid across her skin. Her blood simmered in response and it felt as if she was on fire. She didn't mind the flames at all. She'd been quenching them for five years.

Maybe it was time to fan them instead.

"You're not my boss, Noah. Not anymore."

"Until I get you to change your mind," he said with a satisfied smile that told Tessa he wasn't through trying.

Move, Tessa. Do something, for heaven's sake. Even if it's wrong, do something.

She released a breath she hadn't realized she'd been holding and said, "Just so we're both sure of that..."

She went up on her toes to kiss him.

Dear Reader,

In *Six Nights of Seduction*, you'll meet Noah Graystone and Tessa Parker.

These two were just made for each other. The hard part was convincing them! As Noah's executive assistant, Tessa has been an integral part of his life for five years. As important to him as his phone and his computer—and just as invisible.

Tessa knows she'll never have a life or find love if she's on call for Noah 24/7. But when she turns in her two weeks' notice, Noah is stunned and suddenly can't imagine his life without her. During a business trip to London, Noah tries to tempt her into staying with promises of vacations and raises. But all Tessa wants now is to experience being with him at least once before she says goodbye.

But will six nights be enough? Or will they both risk everything for more?

I really hope you enjoy this story, and please stop by Facebook to say hello!

Happy reading!

Maureen Child

MAUREEN CHILD

SIX NIGHTS OF SEDUCTION

⊕ HARLEQUIN®
DESIRE™

Recycling programs
for this product may
not exist in your area.

ISBN-13: 978-1-335-23286-1

Six Nights of Seduction

Copyright © 2021 by Maureen Child

All rights reserved. No part of this book may be used or reproduced in any
manner whatsoever without written permission except in the case of brief
quotations embodied in critical articles and reviews.

This is a work of fiction. Names, characters, places and incidents
are either the product of the author's imagination or are used fictitiously.
Any resemblance to actual persons, living or dead, businesses,
companies, events or locales is entirely coincidental.

This edition published by arrangement with Harlequin Books S.A.

For questions and comments about the quality of this book,
please contact us at CustomerService@Harlequin.com.

Harlequin Enterprises ULC
22 Adelaide St. West, 40th Floor
Toronto, Ontario M5H 4E3, Canada
www.Harlequin.com

Printed in U.S.A.

Maureen Child writes for the Harlequin Desire line and can't imagine a better job. A seven-time finalist for the prestigious Romance Writers of America RITA® Award, Maureen is the author of more than one hundred romance novels. Her books regularly appear on bestseller lists and have won several awards, including a Prism Award, a National Readers' Choice Award, a Colorado Romance Writers Award of Excellence and a Golden Quill Award. She is a native Californian but has recently moved to the mountains of Utah.

Books by Maureen Child

Harlequin Desire

Tempt Me in Vegas
Bombshell for the Boss
Red Hot Rancher
Jet Set Confessions
The Price of Passion
Six Nights of Seduction

Visit her Author Profile page at Harlequin.com, or maureenchild.com, for more titles.

You can also find Maureen Child on Facebook, along with other Harlequin Desire authors, at Facebook.com/harlequindesireauthors!

To the heroic nurses, aides, doctors and staff
of the George E. Wahlen Ogden Veterans Home
in Ogden, Utah.

I can't thank you all enough for the love,
kindness and care you gave my mother and,
at the end, the rest of us. I've always believed in
angels, and now I can say that I know a lot of them.

A special thank-you goes to Alex, Andrea,
Marcia, Jan, Rose, Linda, Evelyn and Nate.
If I didn't name you personally,
know that I love you.

What you do matters.

One

"Get Matthew on the phone." Noah Graystone flashed a brief glance at his assistant, Tessa Parker. "I want to know how he's doing on getting us that distributor in Michigan."

Tessa made a note on her iPad, then said, "Uh-huh. He's supposed to be calling in at four today to update you."

Noah's gaze lifted to her again and this time, he met her blue eyes steadily. "And we both know he won't. He's a great salesman and good with clients, but checking in on time is not one of my little brother's strengths."

The whole Graystone family was involved in the business—Graystone Fine Spirits—and together, the three of them had built their grandfather's dream into a billion-dollar company. But Noah had long ago accepted that neither his brother nor his sister would ever be quite as committed to the business as he was.

His office, on the top floor of a towering building in Newport Beach, California, boasted views of the harbor and the ocean beyond. Not that he spent much time admiring that view. Usually, he was too focused on his computer screen. Still the office itself was huge and plush, with hardwood floors, rugs in muted colors that picked up the soft gray on the walls. The walls themselves were dotted with framed photos of their distillery, and crowded shelves held awards that their different liquors had won over the years.

But there was one trophy missing. One award that Noah was determined to win. World's Best Vodka in the international competition. Graystone Vodka had been his grandfather's baby. He'd built his company on single malt whiskeys, but vodka was his heart. Now Noah was focused on winning that award in his late grandfather's name. Once he'd done that, he'd move on and win every damn vodka award there was. And nothing was going to stop him.

"Yes, Matthew's a bit loose with his schedules, but you're so rooted in punctuality, you pick up the slack."

His eyebrows rose. "Is that a dig?"

"Possibly," Tessa admitted. She checked her tablet, tapped the screen then said, "Your sister sent an email saying she needs to talk to you about a few promotions she's pushing through."

He waved one hand. His sister, Stephanie, was the COO so he didn't have to be. "Tell her to do what works best for her. I trust her to make the right decisions, besides, I don't have time for another meeting today."

"Okay, and speaking of meetings, the one you can't get out of—with the print company making the new labels—has been moved to three o'clock."

"What?" He dropped back in his chair. Noah's schedule wasn't open to discussion. He expected the people he worked with to have the same focus. "Why?"

"Apparently, Ms. Shipman's babysitter canceled on her. She'll meet with you as soon as her mother arrives to watch the kids."

Kids. Why did people with families insist on also trying to run businesses? *One or the other, people. You can't do both well.* Hell, that was the main reason Noah avoided any kind of commitment to a woman. He'd decided long ago that his focus would be honoring his grandfather. Trying to make right what Noah's own father had practically destroyed.

When he wanted a woman, he had one. But he never considered keeping her around. If that made him a bastard, he thought, well at least he was an honest one.

Shaking his head, Noah muttered, "This is what I get for taking a chance on a small company."

Tessa blew out a breath. "We held a competition to find someone new because our old labeler had gotten stale, remember?"

"I do." That had been his sister Stephanie's idea. They'd received thousands of entries from companies large and small and the publicity had spiked sales for months.

"Well, then, relax and give Ms. Shipman the opportunity to prove you wrong. She has a great reputation and the new logo she came up with is fantastic and you know it."

Scowling, Noah stared at her. Five years she'd worked for him. Had she ever once seen him "relax"? "None of that matters if her kids are keeping her from doing the work."

"They're not. They're simply slowing her down a little today and you're doing it again."

"Doing what?"

She tipped her head and her blond hair swept to one side. "The whole, if-this-doesn't-work-when-I-want-it-to-there's-a-crisis thing."

Noah glared at her and wasn't surprised in the slightest that the look had no effect on Tessa. She'd stopped reacting to his temper after a month on the job, and sometime during the last five years, she'd started actively arguing with him when she thought he was wrong. Not that he was wrong now. Or practically ever.

But Noah had discovered that having Tessa's

honest opinion, even when he disagreed with it, was helpful. Except when it wasn't. Like now.

"Fine. Ms. Shipman at three."

She made a note on her tablet. He pretended he didn't notice the small smile of satisfaction curve her mouth. Noah did that a lot, he realized— avoid looking at Tessa because as her employer he shouldn't be aware of the floral scent of her hair, or the curves he couldn't touch. So, rather than fire her and hire a less distracting and less efficient assistant, pretense was his only option.

Scowling to himself, he said, "Don't forget we're leaving for London in a few days."

"Not likely to forget that," she said.

Neither was he. The international awards for the best spirits of the year included best vodka awards and that was something he would never miss. As far as the powers that be were concerned, Graystone Vodka was the new kid on the block, so the chances of a win were slim. But the contest itself was important, because people would notice them. Talk about them. In next year's contest, he'd have both the varietal and the pure neutral vodka entered and by damn, he promised himself, he'd have that award and he'd lift a glass to his grandfather's memory.

Meanwhile, "Well, there are things I need wrapped up before we leave and the new label is one of them. Ms. Shipman had better show up."

"She will. And it will be done. At three instead of two," Tessa said. Then she added, "I would think you'd be a little more understanding. Callie Shipman's running her late husband's company on her own. She wants to grow it and build something for her family. Sound familiar?"

Noah bit back what he might have said. Of course it sounded familiar. It's what he was doing with the spirits company founded by his grandfather. "The difference is, I keep my appointments."

"And so will she. At three."

Since there was nothing he could do about it anyway, Noah graciously accepted. "Fine. Three."

"And the Barrington hotel in London emailed to confirm our reservations. Your special requests will be taken care of."

"Good." One thing he could always depend on. Tessa Parker would get things done. She might be a distraction at times—like now, for instance. Why did she have to smell so good?—but she was the most organized human he'd ever met. She kept the office running and never missed a step. Hell, he didn't know what he would have done without her the last five years.

"Do you really need the eighteen-hundred-thread-count sheets?" she asked.

He laughed shortly. "If you'd ever tried them, you wouldn't ask."

"Hmm. Is that an invitation?"

He shot her a quick look. "No."

That wasn't flirtation; it was just her sense of humor. Although if she weren't his assistant... Long blond hair, sharp eyes the color of summer skies. Her skin was smooth and pale and she was tall, with more curves than were fashionable at the moment.

And, he told himself firmly, *you're noticing. Stop it.*

"Fine," she said. "The hotel manager also arranged for the car you wanted—though why you had to have an Aston Martin is beyond me."

"James Bond," he quipped and lowered his gaze to the stack of papers on his desk. There was still too much to do before they left for London.

"Right. Of course." He looked up. She tapped her finger against her chin. "Maybe I can get you a meeting with M and Q."

Surprised, Noah stared at her. "You like James Bond?"

"I have two words for you," she said wryly. "Daniel Craig."

"Really. He's your type?"

"Um, let's think. Gorgeous. Built. Strong. And then there's the accent."

He scowled at her, though why it bothered him that she was attracted to some actor, he couldn't have said. "Ah. Well, it's his car I want."

"Of course you do."

"I hear disapproval, but I'm disregarding it."

"Naturally." Tessa took a breath and said, "The Arizona bottler is having an issue, keeping up with the new orders we're sending them."

"That's good news," Noah said. "Means we're

going to need to contract with another bottler soon. Tell Stephanie to start putting out some feelers. I want a few different operations to choose from."

He'd been working for years toward this step up. Family money was all well and good, because damned if it didn't make getting a company up and running easier. But rebuilding Graystone Spirits was the driving force in his life and Noah wouldn't stop until he'd put the company at the top.

"Graystone is going to be bigger than ever." It was a vow, not a statement. "And we'll need companies who can keep up with us."

"I'll tell her," Tessa said.

He looked up at his assistant and asked, "Anything else on the England trip?"

It was important. Not just to Noah personally, but the future of the company.

Graystone had been left to founder the last twenty years, well, until Noah took over ten years before. Since then, he'd been fighting to turn it around. He was on the path now and he wouldn't let anything detour him. One day, he would lift a toast at his grandfather's gravesite and let the old man know that Noah had saved his dream.

While the family fortune had been built on whiskey, Graystone Vodka had been Noah's grandfather's "baby." The old man had dreamed of creating a world-class vodka as a tribute of sorts to his own father. But then his competitive nature had taken over and he'd built their whiskey line into a brand known worldwide and the vodka had taken a back seat. He worked on it when he could and vowed that one day, the vodka would be as popular as their whiskey blends. And it might have happened, but then Noah's father had taken over the reins, and he'd personally ended that.

Jared Graystone had wanted the family money, but hadn't been interested in building it, or in safeguarding the companies that provided him with the lifestyle he loved. Jared hadn't affected most of the businesses because they'd been too protected under the umbrella of a board of directors. But Graystone Vodka had stood alone, a company of the heart for Noah's grandfather. And so it had been easy for Jared to run it into the ground.

He'd drained it of money, allowed employees to drift away, losing distillery masters to greener pastures. Jared had indulged himself in women, hard living and finally had died the way he'd lived. In a car with his latest girlfriend, both of them drunk, sailing off a cliff in Northern California to land in the ocean.

Noah's fingers curled around a pen he snatched off the desk. Even after all these years, he could still feel the surge of anger and shame at the man his father had been.

"Noah?"

He blinked and came out of his thoughts to find Tessa staring down at him, a question in her eyes. "Are you okay?"

"Yeah. I'm fine." He brushed her concern aside and forced himself to stay in the present, and to avoid the past. Ghosts couldn't help him now anyway.

"Ooookaaaayy…" She drew the word out and practically made it a paragraph all on its own. He heard the curiosity in her voice but Noah didn't feel a need to satisfy it. Instead, he kept quiet and waited. Finally, Tessa shrugged and continued, "The jet's being checked over, to get it ready for the flight."

"And?"

"And, your mother called again."

Noah tossed his pen onto the desk and leaned back. His mother was happily remarried and now living in Bermuda and Noah was glad for it. God knew she'd put up with a hell of a lot from Noah's father. She deserved to be happy. But he didn't have the time or inclination to listen to his mom tell him that he was wasting his life, devoting himself to work. To remind him that his beloved grandfather had spent more hours with his company than he ever had with his family. That time was passing and if he didn't do something soon, he'd end up the world's loneliest billionaire.

He wasn't lonely. Hell, he was never alone unless he wanted to be. He had friends. He had women when he wanted them. And as for working too much, hell, he'd never found anything else that could completely captivate him like the company did. There was always another merger or another deal. And mostly, there was the driving desire to build Graystone Vodka into the top brand in the world. And if he had to work twenty-four/seven to do it, then that's what would happen.

"Did she leave a message?"

Tessa checked her notes on the tablet again. "She said and I quote, 'Tell him he can't avoid me forever.'"

He scowled. He wasn't avoiding her per se. He was just busy. Which was, he allowed silently, his mother's point.

"Fine. I'll call her later."

Tessa snorted.

"What was that?"

"We both know you're not going to call her."

"Do we?" he countered.

Tessa held her tablet to her chest and crossed her arms over it. "You don't want to give her the opportunity to tell you to get a life."

"I have a life, thanks," he said.

"Sure you do."

Irritated now, Noah looked up at her. Her features were tightly drawn and she seemed, now that he thought about it, wired pretty tightly. In the five years she'd worked for him, he'd never seen her less than professional. Why the difference today?

"What's going on with you?"

Tessa took a breath and huffed it out. The only way to do this, she told herself, was like taking off a Band-Aid. Do it fast. "I'm trying to figure out how to tell you that I quit."

Frowning, he asked, "Quit what?"

Her eyes rolled. "*My job*, Noah. I'm resigning."

"Don't be ridiculous." He waved that off with a low chuckle.

"I'm not." Tessa watched him, waiting for the reality of what she was saying to hit him. When it finally did, he stared at her as if she had two heads.

"You're serious?"

"Absolutely." This had been building inside her for several months. And she'd finally come to the realization that the only way she would ever find a life for herself was to leave the job—and the man— she loved. The sooner the better.

He shot to his feet. "Why would you do that?"

Well, she couldn't exactly give him the driving reason behind her resignation. She wasn't about to tell him that she'd been in love with him almost the entire time she'd worked for him. How pitiful was that? No, thank you.

So she gave him the secondary reason, which in its way was just as important as the first.

"Because I want time to focus on my own business," she said honestly. "I've got enough money saved now to make it possible for me to work for myself—"

"You have a business?"

Tessa wanted to sigh again, but why bother. She'd mentioned it to him before. Several times over the last couple of years, but if you didn't have *Vodka* stamped on your forehead, he pretty much didn't hear or see you. "Yes, I do. I make lotions and soaps and things and sell them on Etsy and it's recently started taking off. I want to build on that."

He pushed one hand through his dark blond hair and shook his head. "Well, if you've built your business while working for me, why do you have to stop?"

Because she just couldn't face coming into this office every day for the next twenty years and being silently, pitifully in love and having to pretend she wasn't. Because she didn't like making dinner dates for him with some model or actress. She didn't like shopping for gifts for the women who spent the night in his bed so he could send them on with a friendly *thanks but goodbye* note. Honestly, there was only just so much a woman could take.

"Because unlike you, Noah," she said firmly, "I'd like to have a life outside this office."

He stared at her. "You just admitted you *do* have one."

"No." She shook her head. "What I have are bits and pieces of time that I can devote to my work because I'm on call for you twenty-four/seven."

"You're exaggerating."

"Am I? Last Sunday night, where was I?" She didn't wait for him to answer. "I was at your penthouse because you called at eleven thirty to tell me you'd had a brainstorm about the varietal vodkas you want to produce next spring. You needed me to research it to make sure we were coming up with something new and exciting."

He frowned at her. "That was an anomaly."

"Really?" She hitched one hip higher than the other and tapped the toe of her taupe heels against the burgundy carpet. "The day before I was out with a friend and got a text from you saying you needed me to come to the office, pick up the Finnegan file and take it to your place."

She'd been to his home on the cliffs in Dana Point countless times over the last five years. But, Tessa thought, she'd never been upstairs. Never been in his bedroom. To her, it was like the prom-ised land—and she'd likely never see it. Because she'd *never* had him look at her and feel that he was actually seeing *her*.

"It was important. Old man Finnegan was try-ing to hold up the merger and—"

She didn't let him finish. Because the longer she talked to him about this, the more it struck her that she should have quit two or three years ago. Noth-ing would ever change between them and hanging around wishing things were different wasn't help-ing her in the slightest.

"Don't you get it? It's *always* important, Noah. I left my friend at the movies, went to the office to get the file and then spent the next ten hours at your home, *working*." Frowning at the memory, she added, "I ended up napping on the couch in your living room because as much as *you* might be driven, I need sleep once in a while. And I got a crick in my neck for my troubles."

"Is this about your salary?" he countered. "Because I'll give you a raise."

Another sigh. She just couldn't help it. He wasn't getting it and she was pretty sure he was remaining oblivious on purpose. "It's not about the money."

He came around the edge of the desk and stopped when he was only about a foot away from her. For one brief, shining moment, Tessa fantasized that he would come closer, sweep her into his arms and declare undying adoration for her. She almost laughed at herself.

"How about a company car, then?"

"You're not listening to me, Noah. I don't want a car, either."

"What the hell do you want, Tessa?"

"Again, I point out that you're not listening. I already told you. I want a life, Noah. And if I keep working for you, I'll never get one." She looked around the luxurious office and briefly paused to take in the ocean view through the wide windows, before turning back to him. "I'll end up just like you. Only alive within these four walls. No time for friends. For love."

"Seriously?" he asked. "My mother couldn't get to me, but she got to *you*?"

"Believe it or not, I didn't actually need your mother to tell me that finding someone to love is important."

"I'm not stopping you from that," he argued.

Oh, he really was, because *he* was the one she loved, and he was so blind to everything that wasn't Graystone Vodka, he'd never notice her. To him she was an efficient piece of office furniture. A dependable printer. A top-of-the-line computer.

"I don't want to argue with you, Noah. I just want you to know that this is my two-week notice." No point in dragging this out any longer. "If you want me to interview people for my position, I'm happy to do it."

"No." He shoved both hands into his pants pockets. "I'm not going to discuss this further right now. Just…get Finnegan on the line, will you? I need to iron out a few more details."

"Sure." She turned for the door and when she reached it, he said her name and she stopped, then looked over her shoulder at him.

"This isn't over, Tessa."

"Yes it is, Noah."

She left the office and felt like a shipwreck survivor finally reaching shore. Her knees were weak, her heartbeat was racing, but she had to give herself an imaginary pat on the back. She'd done it. She'd actually quit. Now all she had to do was get through the next two weeks.

Because Tessa knew Noah Graystone very well and he wasn't finished trying to get her to stay.

Two

Tessa stopped, took a deep breath and blew it out. That wasn't easy, but she'd done it. And she survived. And now all she had to do was make it through the next two weeks.

Then she'd be free. She'd be running her own business from her home. And she wouldn't have to come here every morning and face a day of being with a man who looked at her and never really saw her. Not that she could blame him entirely, Tessa told herself.

Even if he was attracted to her, he was her boss so couldn't say anything. But she'd been telling herself that for five years and even she didn't believe it anymore. There'd never been the slightest flicker of interest from Noah. So rather than long for a man who would never see her—time to leave.

The phone on her desk was ringing, thank God, so Tessa pushed her own thoughts aside to walk over and answer it. "Noah Graystone's office."

"Hi, Tess!"

Matthew Graystone, calling in, she checked the clock—seven hours early. One thing you could count on with Noah's brother—he was always unpredictable. "Matthew. How's the trip going?"

"Excellent. That's why I need to talk to the boss."

"I'll put you through."

"Thanks."

She rang Noah's office and said, "Matthew's on the phone."

"Hmm. Early for a change."

When she hung up, she dove into work because that was the one thing she could always do to keep her mind busy. But an hour later, she had to admit it wasn't working. Now that she'd finally set her plan into motion, Tessa couldn't stop wondering if she'd done the right thing.

Of course she had. It was just the tiny voice in the back of her mind, taunting her with the knowledge that she'd probably never see Noah again that had her questioning herself. Which was beyond irritating because the reason she was quitting was so she could put some distance between herself and Noah.

Noah had been starring in her dreams for years and it was time to admit those dreams were never going to be reality. *But*, that treacherous voice whispered, *how can you give up what you've never had?*

Frowning, Tessa brought up Noah's schedule for the international vodka awards. While she made corrections and notes for herself, that little voice kept talking, damn it.

Sex, Tessa. I'm talking about sex.

Well, she'd had sex plenty of times. She'd even had a fiancé once upon a time. Until he'd cheated on her with her former best friend. Still, she'd told herself that it was better to find out *before* the wedding that her fiancé was a no-good-lying-cheating dog. And her ex-friend was even worse.

That was one of the reasons she'd left Wyoming for California and a fresh start. Her parents had been happily married forever. Her older brother was married with kids and even her cousins were in relationships or marriages that made her heart hurt at every big family gathering. So she'd packed up and left. Now she only had to hear about what everyone was up to on the phone. She wasn't faced with it all the time.

So sure. She'd had sex.

But not with Noah.

Of course not. He was her boss.

Not anymore.

Her fingers stilled on the keyboard. Did that voice have a point?

Yes.

Her frown deepened, but she couldn't quite dismiss the notion that annoying voice had suggested.

Two weeks and she was gone. Two weeks with Noah and then he would be out of her life. But had he ever really been *in* it? Yes, she'd spent nearly every day for the last five years with him, even the occasional night. But those nights had not been spent the way she would have wanted them.

Maybe sex is what you need.

That voice was really irritating now, because it had a valid point. If she was going to say goodbye to Noah forever, then why not indulge in one night of memorable sex—and she knew it would be memorable, because, well, just look at the man.

Technically, he's not your boss anymore.

True. She *had* quit her job. This two-week thing was just...considerate. There was nothing ethically or legally icky standing between them now.

So, if there's nothing stopping you...what's stopping you?

She sighed and started typing again, but she wasn't paying attention to what was popping up on the screen. Instead, she thought of Noah.

Of seducing Noah.

And damned if she could come up with a reason not to.

Although she had to silently admit, she wasn't trying very hard to talk herself out of it. Why shouldn't she get the one thing she'd dreamed of for five long years before leaving?

"Are you listening to me?" Matthew's voice carried the sting of irritation.

"What?" Noah shook his head and tuned back into the conversation at hand. "Of course I'm listening. You got the distributor in Nashville."

"Try to contain your enthusiasm. It's embarrassing."

"Sorry. Good job." Noah paused, then asked, "Weren't you supposed to be nailing down the Michigan distributor?"

"Yes and I did that. Consider Nashville a bonus," Matthew said. "I got their agreement this morning. Thought I'd tell you right away since we've been after this deal for six months."

"Right." Noah swiveled in his chair and faced the wide window with its view of the ocean. On that expanse of blue, boats with colorful sails skimmed the surface while charter fishing boats chugged far out of the harbor, headed for open sea.

The view should have been soothing. It wasn't.

"Okay, I can only assume you're dying or something. You're never this disinterested in business."

"What?" Scowling fiercely, Noah turned his back on the window and forced himself to focus. "I'm interested. And happy you got both of those distributors nailed down."

"Uh-huh," Matthew said. "What's going on?"

Still frowning, Noah shot a glance at the closed office door. On the other side, he knew Tessa sat at her desk as she had for the last five years. She was the warrior at the gate. No one got past her to see him unless she approved it. She knew the names of every one of the employees here at Graystone Spirits and probably their kids' names, too. She was the one who reminded him about birthday bonuses for the office workers and the one who shopped for his mother at Christmas.

Tessa kept his schedule, ran his life and pretty much managed the whole company; he had to admit that, even if only to himself.

They'd been a damn good team for years and suddenly she decides, *that's enough*? No. he wasn't buying it. There was something else going on here and he would find out what it was.

But his brother was still waiting for an explanation, so Noah blurted out, "Tessa just quit."

"Seriously?" Matthew sounded as stunned as Noah felt and for some reason that made him feel better. "Why?"

"She says she wants a life. What the hell does she have now?"

"A job."

"A damn good job," Noah countered, feeling as if he suddenly had to defend himself as an employer. "She's never complained."

"Right. So you have to ask yourself…what did you do?"

He hadn't considered that. If he'd pissed her off at some point, he had no doubt at all that she would have let him know about it. But as he thought about the question now, all he could come up with was, "Nothing."

"Well, something prompted this, so talk to her.

Try to figure out what went wrong. Hell, Noah. You're the *fixer*. If you can't solve this no one can."

True again, he told himself. Since he was a kid, Noah had been the one to look at a situation and find the best route through it. He never missed a loophole. Never let opportunity slip past him. He could find the lone diamond in a pile of rocks dismissed by everyone else.

"You're right."

"Hell," Matthew said on a snort of laughter, "this phone call was worth it just to hear *that*."

"Yeah, don't get used to it." With thoughts of Tessa worming through the back of his mind, Noah set his subconscious to work on the problem. Meanwhile, though, "Any news on the distributor in Kansas City?"

"And, it's back to business," Matthew mused. "Yeah, I've got a call in to him. Just waiting to hear back. I'm flying out there tomorrow to do an in-person meet and greet."

"Good. Tell me about the Nashville deal." He only half listened as his brother talked, while his mind looked for the solution to the problem of Tessa.

"I did it."

After work, Tessa took a seat at her neighbor's kitchen table and reached for the glass of wine Lynn had already poured. Tessa took a long drink and let the cold, dry wine ease away the sharp edges that had been tearing at her for hours.

Noah had spent most of the day trying to talk her out of resigning. Reminding her about how well they worked together—which she knew. How much they'd accomplished. And the fact that if she left, she would be breaking up the team.

The man was relentless. But in spending all that time with her, he'd only managed to underscore her need to quit. Being with him all the time was just too much. She couldn't take it anymore. Tessa was tired of fighting her attraction to him.

"Well, hey," Lynn said with a grin, "congratulations. Really didn't think you would."

Lynn was five feet two inches tall, with curly black hair, a wide smile and a warm heart. She was the neighborhood "mom" even though she was only thirty-five. Everyone in this part of Laguna knew that if they needed help, go see Lynn.

"Thanks for the support," Tessa said and twirled the stem of her wineglass.

"Oh, come on." Lynn gave her a nudge. "You know I'm on your side. How'd he take it?"

"He offered me a raise."

Lynn laughed. "So typical of men. Toss money at a problem."

Tessa nodded. "He honestly looked stunned when I told him I quit."

"Why wouldn't he be?" Lynn shook her head. "You've been there five years, honey. You do everything for him but trim his hair."

Tessa took a sip of her wine and otherwise kept

her mouth shut. How could she admit that once she actually *had* trimmed his hair? Oh, not a whole haircut, but Noah hadn't liked the wave in his hair and since they were on his jet on the way to a meeting, he'd asked Tessa to trim it. She'd had her fingers in his thick, wavy hair and if she admitted that to Lynn, she'd never hear the end of it.

Every Friday night for the last two years, she and her neighbors had a standing wine-and-snacks date. They traded off locations every week and tonight, thank Heaven, was Lynn's turn. Because her "snacks" were always so much better than the ones Tessa came up with.

She reached out for the plate in front of her, picked up a bacon-wrapped stalk of asparagus and took a bite, just managing to squelch a sigh of approval. There was cheese and crackers—warmed Brie, of course, not the supermarket cheddar Tessa used. Baked chicken tenders on toothpicks and homemade salsa and corn chips.

"What are you thinking?" Lynn asked,

"Just that it's a wonder you and Carol don't weigh five hundred pounds each. You're way too good in a kitchen."

Lynn grinned. "I've even managed to get the kids to eat vegetables. Watch." She turned in her seat and called out, "Jade. Evan."

The girl and boy, ten and eight years old respectively, came running.

Their mom asked, "Want some asparagus?"

"Sure!" Jade grabbed one of the bacon-wrapped stalks and took a big bite. Evan took one, too, unwrapped the bacon and handed the vegetable to his mother. When they left again in a mad rush back to their Disney movie, Tessa laughed.

Wryly, Lynn said, "One out of two isn't bad."

Carol walked in the back door just then, dropped her purse on the kitchen counter and walked straight to the table. Even before she grabbed an empty wineglass, she bent down to kiss her wife hello. "Oh, boy, I'm glad to be home."

She dropped into a chair, poured some wine and snatched a cracker off the plate.

"Busy day?"

"You have no idea," Carol said. "I had a mom's group come in today, with all eleven of their combined children because one of them has the chicken pox. They all wanted the kids looked at—just in case. And I had to tell them that keeping them all together in a herd will pretty much guarantee that they'll all get it."

As a pediatrician, Carol was perfect. She loved kids. It was the parents who frustrated her at times. Her long blond hair was pulled back into a ponytail that hung down her back and her big blue eyes looked tired.

"Don't they have vaccinations for that now?"

"Bingo." Carol pointed her finger at Tessa. "But do people get them? No. You wouldn't believe…"

Lynn held up both hands. "This is officially a

work-free zone," she announced, giving her wife a hard look. "No complaining, either."

"Not even about Colton Briggs biting me again?" Carol shook her head. "Three years old and the kid's got a bite like a Great White."

Lynn laughed, but shook her head. "Not another word until we've all had enough wine that we won't care."

Carol opened her mouth to argue, then shut it again. "You're right, sweetie. Just feed me and keep the wine coming."

Envy whispered through Tessa as it always did when she was with her friends. The two women had the best relationship she'd ever seen. Oh, they argued like anyone else, but they were always there for each other. The love between them was practically palpable. They'd been together nearly fifteen years and they were still so happy.

The kids were in the living room watching a movie, and their laughter drifted to them through the house. Lynn slid the plate of cheese and crackers closer to Carol and said, "She did it."

"Who did what?" Carol took a swig of wine.

"Who do you think?" Lynn said, laughing. "Tessa did it. She actually quit her job."

Carol's eyes went wide. "Seriously?"

Tessa smothered a groan. Was she really so pitiful that her friends were actually proud of her for quitting a job that she had loved for five years?

"God, you guys, it's not miraculous or anything. I just handed in my two weeks' notice. No big deal."

Carol picked up her wine and toasted Tessa with it. "Sure. No big deal. Except you've been talking about doing this for two years."

"I think this is a sign of the apocalypse," Lynn whispered.

"Funny." Tessa grimaced and grabbed another asparagus stalk.

"Oh, come on honey, we're just teasing," Lynn said.

"Yeah," Carol added, "we're just glad you finally did it. Now the trick will be to stick with it."

"I know you're kidding, but come on." Tessa sipped at her own wine. "Of course I'm sticking with it. What would be the point of quitting in the first place otherwise?"

Lynn shrugged. "Noah's not going to give up easily."

True. He would miss having her at his beck and call. Who else could he hire who would put up with working weekends and nights?

"I know, but I've made up my mind."

When both women just stared at her blankly, Tessa argued. "I *have*."

"Prove it," Lynn said.

"How?"

"When he calls this weekend—"

"And he *will* call," Carol tossed in.

"Don't answer," Lynn said. "Or better yet, turn

your phone off completely. Let him get used to not having you to run interference for him all the time."

Tessa thought about that for a moment. It would be weird having her phone turned off, which was probably a bad sign—she was too addicted to the darn thing. But if she didn't and Noah did call—and Carol was right, he would—she would probably cave and answer the phone. What did that say about her? Was she really a glutton for punishment, as her grandmother used to say? "Okay, you have a point, though I am still working for him for the next two weeks…"

"During the week. During the day." Carol's eyes narrowed on her. "Nights and weekends are yours. Supposedly. Even I get every other weekend off."

Tessa took a deep breath. "You're right. I know you're right and that's why I quit and that's also why I'll turn my phone off this weekend."

And to show both of her friends that she was serious, Tessa pulled her phone out of her pocket and shut the power off. Watching it shut down gave her a little pang. Of course, the voice in her head whispered, *But what about emergencies?* No, the only likely "emergency" was Noah wanting her to work on some plan or other. So, better she do this than get sucked into Noah's world again. She had to start distancing herself from him. For her own sanity.

Lynn chuckled. "Are you okay?"

"Not sure yet." Tessa gave her a wry smile. "I'll survive. Probably."

"Here's to you breaking out. Building your own business. And maybe," Carol added as she lifted her glass, "finding a *man*."

The problem, Tessa thought, was that she'd already found the man she wanted. Sadly she couldn't have him.

"Although," Lynn offered, "if you want to spread your wings, I have a friend…"

Tessa laughed and shook her head. "No, I'll stick to men, but thanks anyway."

She wanted of course, to stick to Noah. But that wasn't going to happen.

Then that little voice whispered, *He's not your boss anymore, Tessa. Seduce him before you leave. What do you have to lose?*

Noah had never been to Tessa's house. Hell, he'd had to pull up her information from Human Resources just to find out *where* she lived. Which annoyed him. He should have known, shouldn't he? Tessa had been to his home in Dana Point several times, but he hadn't even been aware that she lived in Laguna. Practically around the corner from him. And he'd had no idea.

He parked by the curb in front of the tiny house and stepped out of the car. Pausing for a moment, he looked up and down the narrow street, taking it all in.

It was a well-settled neighborhood. The trees were old and spread shade across the street from both sides, making a leafy green tunnel. Homes were small and well-tended and seemed to be an amalgam of every type of architectural style. There were mini-Tudors, Craftsman bungalows and even a couple that were starkly modern. Lights shone through windows, basketball hoops stood in driveways and a lone kid whizzed past him on a skateboard.

"It's like being in a Norman Rockwell painting," he muttered, finally turning his gaze on Tessa's house.

Naturally, her home stood out from the rest. It looked like a miniature castle, complete with a turret room and crawling ivy on the gray stones. Of course Tessa wouldn't be living in some ordinary place. He could have seen her in a Spanish style or a Craftsman style with bright colors and uneven lines. What he'd seen of her the last five years, he knew her to be anything but ordinary. Flowers lined the walkway of cobbled stones leading to the front porch, but he barely noticed them as he approached.

This place, he thought, was as far removed from his own home as Mars was from Earth. He glanced around quickly and shook his head.

He preferred his home, of course. Four thousand square feet, rooftop private pool and a wide view of the Pacific. He only saw people when he chose to. On this street, you could be ambushed by neighbors determined to suck up your time and draw you into unimportant conversations.

But he wasn't here to talk to Tessa's neighbors.

He was here to convince Tessa to stay at Graystone. And he didn't care what he had to do to make that happen.

The yard was small but tidy and he idly wondered if she actually mowed the grass herself. Out by his pool, there were potted flowers and trees and even a trellis with some kind of flower crawling all over it. He couldn't remember even *seeing* the gardeners who cared for the gardens at his home. It was just done. Like elves coming in the night. That was just how Noah liked it.

A light shone down on the narrow front porch and highlighted the tumble of flowers and some kind of ivy spilling from a huge terra-cotta pot. The front door was an arch of dark, heavy wood that looked as if it would be at home on a real castle.

The house was more…whimsical than Noah would have expected from someone like Tessa. She was always so pragmatic. So realistic. Seeing this side of her was eye-opening in a way and made him think that maybe he didn't know her as well as he thought he did.

"Ridiculous," he muttered. Of course he knew Tessa. They had spent so much time together over the last five years, he knew her better, apparently, than she did herself. Because he knew she didn't really want to quit. She liked her job. She was good at it.

He knocked firmly on the thick door and waited

impatiently for her to answer. When she did, though, Noah was speechless.

Tessa's blond hair was long and loose around her shoulders. She wore a pale blue T-shirt that clung to her figure in a way that her business attire never did. The hem of the shirt was short enough to display an inch of bare skin above the waistband of her black shorts and when she inhaled sharply, that waistband dipped lower over her belly, sending a hot blast of lust blasting through Noah. Her long legs were bare and her toenails were painted bright scarlet. She looked, he thought…edible.

"Noah?" She stared up at him and confusion shone in her blue eyes. "What're you doing here?"

Was her voice normally that husky or was he just imagining things?

"We need to talk." He pushed past her into the house.

"Please," she said from behind him. "Come in."

Three

Noah stopped just over the threshold and shot her a wry look. Then he took a moment to glance around the interior. Stone walls in the entryway, too, continuing the whole magical cottage feel. There were colorful rugs on the hardwood floors and paintings and framed photographs on the walls.

He kept walking and stepped into a tiny living room filled with an overstuffed couch and twin matching chairs. Tables gleamed from polish and the lamps lit in the room threw a soft, golden glow across the scene that made it all seem…homey, not claustrophobic. Which was impressive since the whole room was about the size of his walk-in closet.

He turned to face her and briefly let his gaze

sweep over this unexpected Tessa. He had to admit, he liked the look. A lot. She swiveled to close the door and he had a half second to admire the curve of her butt and knew he'd never forget it. Reaching up, he briefly rubbed the bridge of his nose hard enough, he hoped, to wake up his brain.

"Why are you here?"

"I already told you," he said. "We have to talk."

"Yes," she said, folding her arms beneath her breasts, lifting them to dazzling heights. "But usually when we 'have to talk,' I get a phone call telling me to drive to your place. Heck I didn't even think you knew where I live."

"Of course I knew." The lie came easily. He wasn't about to admit that he'd had to look up her address. Five years she'd worked for him and her personal life was a blank page. He'd had no idea she was running a business in her "free" time. No idea she lived in a cottage that looked as if it had popped out of a fairy tale.

And zero idea she looked *that* good in shorts.

Not the point.

"Huh." She was surprised, but she accepted what he said. "So again. Why are you here?"

"Like I said, we need to talk."

"About what, Noah?"

"You know what," he snapped and wasn't sure who he was more bothered by. Her? Or himself? Catching her like this, relaxed, casual—tempting— was feeding all sorts of intriguing possibilities in his mind. "You quit, Tessa and I don't accept it. It's ridiculous."

"No it's not. Actually, it's long past time I did," she said and walked past him, heading down a short, narrow hallway as if he wasn't there at all.

Noah followed because what choice did he have? Tie her to a chair? Or a bed? No… "Where are we going?" he asked.

"I'm going to the kitchen and then the garage. I don't know what you're doing."

"Following you." He walked into the kitchen and wasn't surprised to find it a small—he supposed *cozy* was the right word—room. Dark green walls, pale oak cabinets and the same hardwood flooring in here. There was a two-person table sitting under the window and a kitchen island where dozens of small, empty jars sat waiting. For what?

Tessa moved directly to a stove that looked older than she was and picked up a wooden spoon. She stirred the contents of a stainless steel pot and lifted the scent of jasmine into the air.

It was warm in the closed-up room, so Noah slipped out of his suit jacket and walked over to hang it on the back of one of her chairs. "What are you doing?"

She threw a quick glance at him. "I'm making candles."

"Seriously? You make your own candles?" He'd never known anyone who did something like that. "They sell them, you know. Is that what this is about really? A big raise? Do you make your own soap, too?"

"Yes, no, no and yes," she answered all four questions. "I could buy candles but I can make my own. Plus, I'm making these to sell on my Etsy site and third, no, it's not about a raise. I already told you that. And, I already told you I make soaps and lotions."

Had she? He didn't remember.

Once she'd finished stirring the pot, she took the spoon to the island, dripped a bit of melted wax into the bottom of the jars and then affixed a wick to each splotch.

Noah frowned as he watched, but kept quiet. He didn't understand what she was doing, but damned if he wasn't enjoying watching her do it. She moved gracefully, soundlessly, in her bare feet and for some reason, he was really enjoying those bright red toes of hers. When she swung back to the stove, he had another good view of her behind and noticed with interest that there was the hint of a tattoo at the small of her back, just peeking over the waistband of her shorts.

And he instantly wanted to find out what that tattoo looked like.

He undid the button of his collar and loosened his tie.

A few minutes later, she swung her hair back over her shoulder before she picked up a hot pad, then lifted the pot off the stove. He bit back a warning about how dangerous hot wax was, because no doubt she was already aware. Yet still, he kept quiet as she poured the wax into the waiting jars, adjusting the wicks so that they remained straight as she poured. She filled six jars before she was finished, propped up the wicks with what looked like chopsticks, then turned and set the pot back on the stove.

Finally, he asked, "How do you get the rest of the wax out of the pot?"

"I don't," she said. "I'll reheat this for the second pour once this pour sets up."

"Second pour?" Why was he interested? Because she was talking and he was watching her mouth move and wondering why he'd never noticed how full her bottom lip was.

She sighed. "The first pour will settle and a sort of concave will open up along the wicks. The second pour will correct it."

"Okay." He didn't really care. He just wanted to keep watching her.

"Whatever residual wax is left over will become part of the remelt in a couple of days. This is my jasmine pot and I'll use it again for more candles then."

"Remelt." Noah shook his head and watched her set the pan down on one of the front burners.

"That's right. I've got to go to the garage. I'll be back in a minute."

He wasn't going to stay behind and look like an idiot alone in her kitchen, so he followed and enjoyed the view of her butt as he walked behind her. The edges of that tattoo kept drawing his gaze and he wondered what it was. Dolphin? Rainbow? Mermaid? Hmm.

Noah shook his head. Tattoo aside, he approved of the view of her behind. Somehow, Tessa had managed to camouflage her really amazing butt beneath business suits and skirts, and he never would have guessed she would have a tattoo. This was a nice surprise…and a little unsettling. He didn't like what looking at her was doing to him, but there didn't seem to be much he could do about it.

A breeze shot up out of nowhere and still did nothing to ease the heat building inside him. Noah scowled, stuffed his hands into his pockets and glanced around at the darkened yard as they walked to the garage.

Small again. Surprising, really that she could have so many flowers and trees in such a tiny space. Everything was neatly tended and he imagined that in summer, the explosion of flowers would be spectacular. Even now, there were flowers with dusky colors dotting the garden line.

Tessa opened the side door to the garage, flipped a switch and a sword of light pierced the gathering darkness. He followed it like a path and stepped inside behind her.

Again, surprise had him stopping in place to look around. Now he understood why her car was parked in the driveway.

This wasn't really a garage, he told himself, it

was more of a workshop. There were two sturdy tables set up in the middle of the room with boxes stacked neatly at the ends of both of them. Along the walls were shelves, neatly arranged with boxes of glass jars, and gallon-sized jugs filled with pastel-colored liquids and other shelves holding huge boxes of who knew what? Stacked neatly on the floor were several more jugs filled with a milky fluid. And what looked like a tension rod between cabinets held roll upon roll of ribbons.

"What is all this?" he asked, a little dumb-founded.

"My business," she said from the corner where she was dipping into one of the mystery boxes. She came up with a single white block about ten by eight and two inches thick, broken up into small squares. "I store my candle wax, scents and lotion bases out here. And I use the tables to fill big orders."

"When do you have time for all this?" he wondered aloud before he could stop himself.

A wry smile curved her mouth and he found the motion...tantalizing.

"Good question," she said. "I work whenever I can, stealing a few minutes here and there. I don't have enough time to devote to my business. Which is the reason I resigned. Remember?"

He frowned. "You'd rather work in a garage than work for me."

"I'd rather work for myself, yes." She nodded firmly and headed for the door.

When she got close enough, he reached out and grabbed her arm, dragging her to a stop. The instant he touched her, Noah felt a blast of something desperate and undeniable shake him. What the hell was happening?

He'd worked with Tessa for years and but for the occasional moment, he'd paid no attention at all to the fact that she was gorgeous and seriously built. Now it seemed that was *all* he could see. Or think about.

He let her go quickly, but the burn sizzling his fingertips remained.

"We could work something out," he blurted out, staring into her eyes. Were they always such a deep, rich color?

"Noah, it wouldn't work." She took a breath and he absolutely did *not* notice her full breasts rise and fall with the action.

"You can't know that," he argued.

"Please. Who would know better?" She took a tighter grip on the block of wax. "I can't be on call for you twenty-four/seven and still find the time for my own stuff. I've been trying for five years and it doesn't work."

He took the wax from her and was slightly surprised at how heavy it was. "Now that I know you've got this business—" he broke off and gave her a hard look "—which you could have told me about long before now—we can make the time."

She smiled slightly and shook her head. "That's sweet. You might even mean it…"

"I don't say things I don't mean," he said, interrupting her.

"…but it wouldn't last," she went on as if he hadn't spoken. "Noah, you're so focused on your own work, that's all you see."

Not at the moment, he thought, letting his gaze briefly drop to the impressive cleavage she was displaying in that V-neck shirt. Right now, work was the furthest thing from his mind.

"In spite of the fact that I give it so little time, my business is growing. And now I'm also selling jewelry that my neighbor makes, so I'm expanding. I need the time, Noah. So thanks, but I made the right call." She turned for the door and Noah walked right behind her.

Quietly fuming, frustration bubbling inside him, he switched off the light, closed the door behind him and followed her back to the house. The heat of the kitchen was a distinct difference to the chill outside and yet it was *nothing* compared to the heat flaring inside him.

Noah set the block of wax on the tiny island then watched as Tessa reheated the wax she'd been working with before. "What are you doing now?"

"I'm getting the second pour ready," she murmured without bothering to turn and look at him.

Ridiculous as it sounded, he wasn't used to her ignoring him. He didn't much care for it, either.

"How many pours are there?" he asked.

"Usually two, but you can do more. All depends on how the wax settles and what you're looking for."

He glanced at the candles and saw she had been right. The wax was settling, sinking. He'd never thought about candles. Why would he? But now he could see how much work went into such a simple product. Give him the liquor business any day.

Distilleries that worked seamlessly, employees who handled any problems instantly. He knew his way around the business world. He was damn good at it. And he hated to admit it, but Tessa was one of the reasons for his success. His spine stiffened. He couldn't lose her.

He *wouldn't* lose her.

And he would start by tempting her with what mattered most to her—her business.

"You know, if you stayed," he said and paused until she turned to glance at him.

Those eyes of hers captured him again and Noah almost lost his train of thought. Unheard of. He prided himself on his ability to focus on the situation at hand and suddenly, being around Tessa was scattering his thoughts.

"Yes?" she asked, waiting.

Scowling, he muttered, "We could do something about your work setup."

She laughed shortly. "Could we now?"

Noah frowned again, but she didn't see it as

she'd already dismissed him and turned her attention back to the pot she was stirring gently.

"I'll remodel your garage," he said abruptly.

"What? Why?" Now she turned to stare at him wide-eyed.

"Seriously?" He walked closer to her but stopped soon enough to keep a safe distance between them. "You want to grow your business, but you're working in this claustrophobic kitchen and a garage that's already stuffed to the gills. How can you expand if your space is limited?"

She sighed loud enough for him to hear it. "Expanding my business will be as easy as having more time for it, Noah. I'm not trying to be the biggest candle/lotion/soap supplier on the West Coast."

Well, that statement went against everything he'd been taught about business. If you were going to do something, then you should damn well shoot for the top. Be the best. Be the *only*, if you could.

"Why not?" he demanded. "Why wouldn't you want to be the best and the biggest?"

She turned her head to look at him. "We're not *all* as driven as you are, Noah. What I want is for my business to support me and maybe a little extra. Not everyone wants to be a tycoon. Some of us even want to have a life, too."

"I have a life."

She snorted derisively and his scowl turned fierce.

"Not that I've seen," she said and picked up the

pot. Carrying it to the island, she carefully poured a stream of hot, scented wax into each candle, one at a time. The air in the kitchen was suddenly alive with the scent of jasmine. It was thick and warm and, damn it, seductive.

When she set the pot down on the stove again, she faced him and put her hands at her hips. The action tugged the material of her shirt tighter, highlighting those breasts he couldn't seem to stop noticing.

"Noah, I appreciate your self-interested offer of generosity, but I don't need it. I'm happy working out of my kitchen."

"Even if the offer includes a commercial-grade stove and all the equipment you might need to run your business more efficiently?"

She paused, considering, and he knew he'd caught her interest at least. But then she spoke and he knew he'd lost her just as quickly.

"I don't have room here for a commercial-grade stove."

"We'll remodel your kitchen."

Tessa laughed then and shook her head. "I resigned, Noah. It's not the end of the world. You'll get on fine with a new assistant."

No, he wouldn't, damn it. Tessa knew his company as well as he did. Where was he supposed to find that? "No. It'll take years to break her in."

"Or down," she muttered.

"What was that?" he asked, though he'd heard the guttural comment.

"Nothing." She lifted one hand and waved her own comment away. "I only meant that I've done my job and now it's time to do something else."

"Sure." Broke her down? Had he done that? He didn't see how that was possible, since the woman rarely treated him with any kind of deference. She ran his office. Hell, she ran his *life*. No. He wasn't going to accept her words without countering them.

"How in the hell can you say I broke you down?" The question hung in the scented air between them and simmered there for a long minute or two before she answered.

"I'm not getting into this, Noah. Not now."

"Well, you quit your job," he argued hotly, "so if not now, *when*?"

"Does *never* work?" she quipped and his eyes narrowed on her.

Her own fault, Tessa told herself.

She never should have let him in the house. But he hadn't given her a choice on that. And she certainly shouldn't have let him stay. Or muttered that comment just loud enough for him to hear it.

Tessa's kitchen felt incredibly small right now. Normally, the room was perfect. It held memories of her grandmother, whose house it had been. When her grandma died, she'd left the house to Tessa, because she was the grandchild who'd loved it most.

Her family had come to visit Grandma nearly every summer and this house brought every one of those memories to life.

It was big enough for Tessa and her business and she liked that the kitchen was cozy. It made her feel… safe. But tonight, Noah's presence had shrunk the space until she couldn't draw a breath without the essence of him filling her. She hardly detected the jasmine—only his aftershave, a woodsy blend that had always smelled like heaven to her.

And that was totally beside the point—and yet one more reason why she'd quit her job.

Her heart was pounding and her mouth was dry. Completely normal. She was so accustomed to her body, her emotions and her thoughts jittering whenever he was near, it didn't even surprise her anymore. But having him level his laser-like focus on her was brand new and a little unsettling. His blue eyes seemed darker, bigger, somehow, and the way he was clenching his jaw made her wonder what exactly he was thinking.

She had to say something, though, so she started talking. "Maybe that was a little harsh," she said. "It wasn't so much breaking me down as *wearing* me down. I don't want a job where I'm always on duty, Noah."

"You're not."

"Really?" She spread her hands out as she looked up at him. "Because it's Friday night and here you are. In my kitchen."

His frown deepened and Tessa wondered why it was that that expression always seemed more endearing than forbidding.

"I'm not asking you to do any work," he argued.

He was asking her to stay, though, and she couldn't do that. Heck, she'd be mortified to tell Lynn and Carol that her resignation hadn't even lasted twenty-four hours. But it wasn't just that. This was for Tessa's own sake. She needed to find a future that didn't include Noah. If nothing else, his visit here tonight had proven that.

Just being this close to him was driving her crazy. Normally, at the office, she could push aside what she was feeling because it was inappropriate. Boss-assistant attraction was so clichéd even she couldn't stand it. But he was here now. In her space. And he was so close that the temptations she'd fought for so long were rising to the surface, refusing to be ignored.

But ignore them she would.

Why ignore me? that voice whispered almost instantly. *Indulge me instead.*

"Sure you are," she argued, resisting the lure of that voice. "You're trying to bribe me to stay in a job I already quit."

"*Bribe* is a strong word."

"Really?" She had to laugh because Noah could go over the top easily and never realize it. "You just offered to remodel my garage and my kitchen and stock it with top-of-the-line equipment."

"Well," he snapped, "have me shot at dawn for offering to make your life easier."

She sighed. "That's not what I'm saying, Noah, and you know it."

"I thought I knew *you*," he said. "I'm just realizing that I was wrong about that."

Well, good. She was happy to have surprised him at last. Even though it meant having him here, breathing her air, smelling wonderful, radiating enough heat that her skin felt as if it were sizzling.

No, he didn't know her at all. If he did, he wouldn't have come here when she was feeling the rush of leaving her job. When she knew that she didn't have to be circumspect in how she treated him anymore. Because he wasn't, technically, her boss anymore.

So isn't it nice that he's here?

No, it wasn't.

Honestly, that inner voice was getting extremely annoying. Mostly because its whispers were becoming more and more tempting.

"Hello? Earth to Tessa," he said and Tessa realized she'd been thinking too much and talking too little.

"I'm just busy, Noah. I don't have time to go over all the same territory again and again." *Good. Get him to leave.*

Ask him to stay.

"Maybe I can help."

"What?" She goggled at him. The master of his universe wanted to step down into the real world, however briefly, and work in a tiny kitchen? "You want to help me make candles?"

"Doesn't look that difficult," he said with a shrug. "And while we work, we can talk some more."

"Fantastic."

Or, you could forget about the candles and do something else.

"Okay fine," she said abruptly, in an effort to silence that tiny voice inside, "candles it is. There's a walk-in pantry right over there." She pointed to a door in the corner of the kitchen. "Just grab one of the melt pans off the bottom shelf."

"Any one at all?"

"Yeah. We'll make whichever one you choose."

She watched him go and admired the view as she had been doing for five long years. Honestly, no man should have a butt that good. And his long legs, narrow hips, flat stomach and broad chest? Deadly. Really.

What are you waiting for, Tessa?

A sign maybe? A meteor? Asteroid crashing into earth?

He bent down to get one of the pans and Tessa sighed. This was going to be a very long evening.

An hour later, the kitchen was a mess, four new jars of cranberry candles had been filled and Noah was peeling hardened red wax from his five-hundred-dollar shirt. Perfect.

"I'll pay for the shirt," she said.

"Why should you pay for it?" he muttered darkly. "I'm the one who splashed the damn wax."

"You said it didn't look difficult."

"It isn't. It's just…" he frowned. "Dangerous."

Tessa moved in closer, batted his hands away and took over for him. With her fingernails, she could get at the wax still clinging to the fabric. And this close to him, she couldn't avoid dragging his scent into her lungs, or the heat pumping from his body. She heard his every breath and swore she could also count the beats of his heart. When they sped up suddenly, she was sure of it.

Slowly, she straightened, lifted her chin until she could look him in the eye. What she saw there startled that inner voice into shrieking, *This is it, Tessa. Time to make a move.*

Noah's eyes darkened and somehow, at the same time, lit with a heat that she felt burning inside her, too. He lifted one hand and smoothed a strand of her hair back from her face and the tips of his fingers slid across her skin like a wish. Her blood simmered in response and it felt as if she were on fire. She didn't mind the flames at all. She'd been quenching them for five years.

Maybe it was time to fan them instead.

"You're not my boss, Noah. Not anymore."

"Until I get you to change your mind," he said with a satisfied smile that told Tessa he wasn't through trying.

Do something, Tessa. Even if it's wrong, do something.

So she did. She released a breath she hadn't realized she'd been holding and said, "For right now, you're not my boss."

"No," he agreed. "I'm not."

"Just so we're both sure of that." She went up on her toes to kiss him and that voice inside was blessedly silent.

Four

Tessa stunned him.

She felt his shock when she hooked her arms behind his neck and laid her mouth over his. But it was astonishing how quickly he recovered from his surprise. In an instant, his arms came around her middle and pinned her to him as he kissed her back.

It was everything she'd thought it would be. Everything—and more than her dreams had conjured. His mouth was firm and soft and oh, so expert. Her nipples tingled, pressed against his chest so tightly. Her breath caught in her lungs and she didn't mind. Who needed to breathe?

Tessa gave herself up to the moment, letting it fill her and tempt her with the promise of more. The surge of emotions was tangled and confusing, so she ignored them and concentrated on sensation alone. His hands swept up and down her back, cupped her butt and squeezed until she groaned into his mouth.

The sound must have tripped a switch inside him, because Noah tightened his grip on her, swung her around and pressed her up against the refrigerator. Through the heat pulsing inside her, she didn't even feel the sting of cold metal. Seconds ticked past and the only sound was the hard thumping of their hearts. His tongue swept into her mouth and she gasped at the electrifying feeling that jolted through her.

She'd opened Pandora's box here and she wasn't sure what to do next. When he slid one hand up to cup one of her breasts, she at first sighed, enjoying the moment she'd spent so much time dreaming about. But then reality reared its ugly head, her brain woke up and she knew she needed to stop. Think.

No thinking!

The opportunity is right here in front of you. Grab it.

But she couldn't. Not when she had to face him at work for the next two weeks.

Deliberately, Tessa pulled her mouth from his, then pushed out of the circle of his arms. Her knees were weak and her sense of balance was completely gone. If she hadn't slapped one hand down on the kitchen island she might have tipped over.

"What?" Frowning, Noah took a step closer to her. "What the hell, Tessa? Why'd you stop?"

She held up her free hand and took a couple of deep breaths. It wasn't going to help. Nothing would help. *An orgasm might.* But that wasn't going to happen, she insisted silently.

"Because," she finally managed to say, "I promised myself I couldn't leave my job without doing that at least once. And now I have. So, I'm done."

"Uh-huh." He scrubbed one hand across his mouth. "You're done." His breath came as fast and sharp as hers. "You know, there are lots of other things we could do—at least once…"

Oh, boy. There was literally nothing she wanted more. The very idea of being with Noah, naked bodies tangled together on cool, smooth sheets, was enough to make her breath hitch. But resolutely, she shook her head and said, "We still have to work together for the next two weeks, Noah."

"We're not working now," he pointed out.

"No, we're not," she said. "So maybe you should go."

He looked surprised again—not in a good way, this time.

"Seriously?" One eyebrow lifted. "You kiss me like that and then tell me to go?"

"Yeah. Sorry." Boy, she was sorry. Sorry she'd stopped. Sorry they weren't going to go to her bedroom. Sorry she now had to spend the next two weeks thinking about that kiss.

Nodding grimly, he said, "All right. I'll leave."

No. Don't let him leave. What are you thinking?

That inner voice had a point.

He walked over to the chair where he'd hung his jacket a couple of hours ago, shrugged it on, then came back to her. For a moment, Tessa thought he might even lean in to kiss her again, but then she realized he would never do that, now that she'd called an end to it.

"I'm going," he said. "But I'll see you on Monday."

"Right. Monday." Which meant she still had Saturday and Sunday to get past this. Sure. She could do that.

Noah moved in, cupped her cheek in the palm of his hand and tipped her face up so that their eyes met and held. "You will be there, right?"

She blinked at him. "Of course I will."

Nodding, Noah smiled briefly. "Good. Wouldn't want you to chicken out."

Chicken out of what? Facing him? Leaving him? Either way, Tessa was a little insulted even though she knew he was playing his own game. In challenging her, he was making sure that she'd show up. That she wouldn't phone in her last two weeks.

"I don't chicken out."

"Really?" His mouth quirked. "Seems like that's exactly what you just did."

She didn't like the sound of that, but maybe he had a point. "I just came to my senses, is all."

"Yeah, I don't think that's it."

Frowning, Tessa whispered, "You don't scare me, Noah."

"Glad to hear it." He nodded. "Scaring you is the last thing on my mind right now." He left then and from halfway down the hallway, he called back, "See you Monday, Tessa."

Sighing, she sort of slumped against the kitchen island and felt the cold of the granite bite into that inch or so of bare skin at the small of her back. It was a good wake-up call, she told herself. Didn't do anything for the heat still crawling through her body, but the touch of cold was enough to draw her out of the semitrance state that kiss had left her in.

You missed your chance.

"Come on, Tessa," she muttered out loud. "Finish up these candles, then clean up and drink some wine. A lot of wine. And maybe a cold shower."

Cold shower. That's pitiful.

"Be quiet," she snapped to that voice and wondered if it was a bad sign that she was now apparently arguing with herself.

It was a long weekend.

Noah had spent far too much time thinking about that kiss in Tessa's kitchen. He'd tried to brush it off as just a kiss. Nothing special. But even he wasn't believing his lies. Tessa had starred in his dreams and haunted his thoughts for the last two days and he hoped to hell she'd had a bad weekend, too.

Only fair, since she was the one who'd started—and ended it.

On Monday, he got to the office early as per usual.

What was *unusual*? He wasn't on the phone or going over paperwork or even plotting his next move in his quest for worldwide vodka domination. Instead, he was still thinking about Tessa. Waiting for her to arrive. Wanting to see if she'd brushed off that kiss or if it had tormented her as it had him all weekend.

It took a lot to surprise Noah. He prided himself on always being one step ahead of his competitors and even his friends. His long-range thinking had stood him in good stead for years.

Until Tessa kissed him.

He pushed away from his desk and paced to the bank of windows overlooking the Pacific. Staring out at the water and the heavy gray clouds gathering on the horizon, Noah instead saw Tessa's big blue eyes staring up at him. The passion shimmering there had spiked something inside him that he hadn't expected.

Desire, hot and thick, had pumped through his veins and when she'd called a halt, Noah's entire body went from need to frustration in a blink of time. And there he'd stayed all weekend. He hadn't been able to stop thinking about her and when he tried to sleep, she was there, too. In his dreams, smiling at him, opening her arms to him as she tumbled onto his bed.

"At least once," he muttered and pushed back the edges of his suit jacket to shove both hands into his slacks pockets. "So that's good enough for her? Just one kiss?"

Muttering under his breath now, Noah admitted that he didn't like this at all. The kiss, of course he'd liked. He would have had to have been a dead man not to enjoy that kiss—and probably even death wouldn't have been enough to dull the fire Tessa had caused.

What he *didn't* like was the fact that he'd thought about her all weekend and was still thinking about her now. Tessa was a distraction—a hell of one, if he were being honest. And he couldn't risk being distracted now. He couldn't afford to take his eyes off the prize.

Noah was closer now than ever to achieving what he'd been working toward for years. He had a duty to his late grandfather. To the rest of his family and he wouldn't step away from that. Not for anything. Not even for another taste of Tessa.

His hands curled into fists at his sides and Noah fixed his gaze on the ocean and the cloud-swept sky. But as he stared, his mind raced with images from his past.

His father, Jared, had taken over the family company and nearly driven the vodka division into the ground. His father, Thomas, Noah's grandfather, had watched as his son threw away family duty—to the company, to his wife and children—in favor of fast women and even faster cars. Noah was ten when his father left them. And fourteen when a drunk Jared finally drove one of his cars off a cliff, killing himself and his latest woman. It was almost a relief.

Noah's grandfather, an old man, had taken over the reins of the company again, but his heart wasn't in it. He'd taken Noah to work with him, showing him the business, teaching him and basically being more of a father than grandfather. Noah had taken it all in. He'd wanted then so much to make up for what his father had done, he'd promised his grandfather that when he grew up, he'd make Graystone the best in the world.

As memories faded and the present rushed in, Noah gritted his teeth in frustrated anger that hadn't abated over the years. His own father had lost everything in his relentless pursuit of women. Noah had no intention of making the same mistakes.

He was focused on the company. The family. His duty was to build on his grandfather's dream and somehow, some way, erase his father's sins.

Not even Tessa could sway him from that goal.

So during the hours he'd spent thinking of and dreaming of Tessa, Noah had decided over the weekend that this morning, he would act as if nothing had changed between them. He put that kiss, that night, down to a momentary brain blip.

"And now I'm back." He took a deep breath, let his gaze focus on the ocean and told himself that he was unchanged. Unaffected.

"I'm also lying," he muttered, but if there was one thing he'd learned when starting out in business…don't let anyone see you doubt yourself.

So he was prepared when Tessa walked into the office and said, "Good morning, Noah."

"Tessa." He glanced at her. She was wearing one of her conservative suits, this one in a subtle blue with a white shirt and sensible black heels. Her long hair was pulled up into a messy bun that only made him want to free the whole mass and watch it tumble over her shoulders. Grimly, he nodded before returning his gaze to the window and the view beyond. "Work up a schedule for London, will you? I want to know exactly where we'll be and what's happening every day."

"Sure. I'll have it for you in a couple of hours."

"That works." Still not looking at her because how could he? Now he knew what kind of body was hiding beneath that unimaginative blue suit. He knew the toes hidden in those black heels were painted a deep red. And he knew she had a tattoo that was completely camouflaged by the persona of "perfect personal assistant."

No, if he looked at her again right now, he'd be thinking about that night at her place. That kiss. And he'd already vowed to wipe it from memory.

"Anything else?" she asked.

So many things, he thought, but didn't say. "Yeah. Ask my sister to come in when she's free. I've got a few things I want to go over."

"Sure. Is that it?"

"Yes," he said and silently, he added, *just leave*.

"Okay." She didn't leave, though. He could sense her there. Waiting.

Finally, Noah turned to face her and just looking at her made him want to rethink his whole plan.

"Is everything all right, Noah?" She tipped her head to one side and in her eyes, he read confusion.

"Everything's fine." His voice was clipped and as neutral as he could keep it.

She studied him for a long minute. "Should we talk about what happened on Friday?"

"No." One word. Deliberate. He headed for his desk, effectively dismissing her. If he looked at her again, he might lose his resolve.

"I think we should," she said. "It's clearly bugging you."

He looked at her, locking his eyes with hers. Bugging him? No. What bugged him was that he could be so easily drawn off the path he'd laid out for himself. And he wouldn't let it happen again.

"You're wrong, Tessa," he said.

"I don't think so, Noah," she answered, shaking her head. "I was there. I remember. And you do, too."

Oh, yeah. He remembered. Not that he wanted to, it was only that the kiss itself, that moment in time, had been burned into his memory so deeply, he'd never be able to shake it.

But that didn't mean he couldn't ignore it.

"It was a simple kiss. Don't make more of it than there was."

"Don't make less of it, either."

"We're not talking about this," Noah said.

"Funny. Sounds like we are."

He gave her a hard scowl and wasn't the slightest bit surprised when it had no effect on her at all. "We both have work to do," he snapped. "Let's get on it."

"Right. We'll do that." She turned for the door and paused on the threshold. Looking back at him, she added, "But we both know you're lying, so don't think you're getting away with something."

She closed the door a moment later, as if to make sure she got the last word. And Noah had to admit, it had been a good one.

Tessa took the extra time to walk down to Stephanie Graystone's corner office at the opposite end of the floor. Yes, she could have called, but she needed the movement. As if she could walk off Noah's reaction—or non-reaction. Who did he think he was kidding, anyway?

Over the weekend, Tessa had imagined all sorts of ways the conversation with him would go this morning. Some of them had ended with him locking his office door, lying her down on the sofa and—

She broke that thought off quickly. One thing she

didn't need was to indulge an imagination that had been on overdrive since Friday night. Heck, she'd spent most of the weekend working in her kitchen and every moment of that time reliving the kiss. The feel of his arms around her. The hard slam of his heart against hers. And mostly, the wild, over-whelming taste of his mouth fused to hers.

And her dreams had been off-the-chart erotic. She woke up horny and aching and exhausted.

Then he tried to tell her it was nothing? Did he think she was stupid? Was *he* stupid?

Who cares if he's stupid? that little voice shrieked. *He's a hell of a kisser—let's see how good he is at the main event.*

Well, yes, she would really like to, but she'd need his cooperation, damn it.

Tessa barely saw the people she passed. Every-one was at their desk, working busily, while she was fighting raging hormones and a rising temper. The office was huge, open and filled with sunlight through the wide bank of windows overlooking the Pacific. Of course the windows were tinted, but still the light and the view made this a beautiful office to work in. Tessa stared straight ahead, though, down the hall to Stephanie's closed door.

When she got there, she looked at Steph's assis-tant, Angie. "Is she free?"

"Sure," the woman said. "She just got off a call and her next meeting isn't for half an hour."

"Great, thanks." Tessa opened the door, peeked in and said, "Stephanie? You have a minute?"

"I'd love a break. Come on in." Stephanie Graystone was tall—nearly five feet ten inches and was, to put it bluntly, gorgeous. Her dark blond hair was pulled back from her face by a simple headband and then fell past her shoulders in thick waves. She wore a white dress shirt, black slacks, and her black jacket was hung over the back of her chair. Her eyes were a darker blue than Noah's—almost violet, really—and her wide mouth was curved in a smile.

"What's up, Tess?"

"Noah needs to see you, he said. I'm guessing it's something about plans for while we're in London…"

Stephanie's eyebrows lifted into perfectly sculpted arches. "And you had to walk down here to tell me?"

"No," Tessa said and dropped into one of Steph's visitor chairs. The two women had long ago developed a friendship that went beyond employer/employee and today, Tessa was grateful. "I just needed to walk."

"Ah." Stephanie sat back in her chair and swiveled it a little. "Noah's aggravating you, too?"

"Too?" Tessa echoed. "What's he doing to you?"

"Oh, treating me like it's my first week on the job." Stephanie waved one hand gracefully in the air, as if dismissing her older brother. "It's okay—I'm used to it. I hear him out and then do things my way. Keeps us both happy. He is a major con-trol freak after all."

"True." Noah thought that only *he* could run the company the way it should be run. He kept his finger on the pulse of every department and personally oversaw every decision. Well, that wasn't entirely fair. His department heads made their own calls, but Noah wanted to know about them.

"What's going on, Tessa?"

"Nothing." She shook her head, wondering why she'd come to Stephanie. Sure, they were friends, but Noah, no matter how aggravating, was still the other woman's brother. And even when Tessa's brother Joe irritated her beyond belief, she would still stand up for him to everyone else.

"So, what's bugging you?" Stephanie asked.

"I quit on Friday—did he tell you?"

"Yes." Frowning a little, Stephanie said, "He told me Friday evening before he left for the night. He was outraged that you would leave the company."

Outraged. That about covered it. "Are you?"

"No." Stephanie grinned and shook her head. "If you've got a business you want to build, you'll never do it if you're dancing attendance on the king."

Tessa snorted and some of the tension lessened in her chest. "Thanks."

"No problem. But, is there an issue with Noah about this? Is he giving you a hard time?"

I wish.

Oh, stop it, she warned that voice in her mind. That was a terrible pun.

"He did come over on Friday to try to talk me out of it, but he eventually dropped it and helped me make some candles. But it's not about my resignation. Well," she corrected, "not entirely."

Steph smiled slowly and leaned forward. "Ooh. There's a story here. Do I get to hear it?"

"Probably," she admitted. "But first, I've got a question for you that is wildly off topic, but it's something I've been trying to understand for years."

"Now I'm curious. Ask."

"Okay," Tessa said. "I want to know why Noah is so driven. Why does this vodka award mean so much to him?"

"A long story that I'm going to try to cut down to size," Stephanie said on a sigh. "It goes back to our father. First you have to know that dear old dad was just no good at all. He took over for our grandfather—who was already raising us along with our mom because father-of-the-year dumped us."

Tessa winced and immediately compared her own amazing parents to what Steph, Noah and Matthew had grown up with.

"Anyway," Stephanie continued, "it broke Papa's heart to see what his son became and it was hard to watch the old man sort of shrink into himself in response. Noah was the oldest, so he just naturally assumed the obligation to make Graystone what it was before our dad wrecked it.

"Like I said, our grandfather took in Mom and all of us. Gave us a home. And a legacy to live up to." She smiled a little, remembering her grandfather. "Matthew's a lot like our dad without the whole 'terrible human' thing and Noah is practically a clone of our grandfather. Family, duty, matter most to him. I don't think he'll ever give up until Papa's dreams become reality."

Tessa was listening, and didn't like it. Oh, at last she understood what was behind Noah's focus, but that didn't make her feel any better.

Yes, he was driven, successful and focused on the prize he could see right in front of him. But what, she wondered, would he do when he finally *won* that prize? When he met his goal? Would he try for a life then, or would he just shift his focus to the next challenge?

"Speaking of tangents," Stephanie said softly, "I'm actually looking forward to Noah being in London for a week."

"Why?"

"Don't sound so judgmental," Stephanie teased. "It's nothing drastic. But while he's gone, I'm giving everyone three or four days off so I can get painters in here to change the boring, snow-blind white walls and I'm having hardwood floors laid to give the place warmth."

"In three or four days?"

Stephanie winked. "It's amazing what the word *bonus* will get you."

Tessa laughed. "On the way to your office I was thinking this is the most beautiful place to work I'd ever seen."

"Well, sure, we have the ocean view, so that really helps. But come on." Stephanie rolled her eyes. "Let's face it. Noah wouldn't notice his surroundings if they were on fire. But why should the rest of us put up with his bland decorating style? Nope. COO here and I'm making an executive decision. Or two."

"You know what?" Tessa said. "You're right. Noah wouldn't notice unless the Graystone label was splashed across the walls. Go for it, Steph. And text me a picture of it once it's done."

"That's right." Stephanie's shoulders slumped. "You won't be here to see it. And now I'm sad. Who will I complain to about Noah?"

"You can always call me," Tessa offered. She probably shouldn't want to get reports on him as much as she did.

"I may take you up on that," Stephanie said. Then she was quiet for a moment or two before blurting, "You know, Tessa, you should just go for it."

"It?"

"Noah. I mean you won't see him again after London. You've been in love with him forever. So seduce him."

"You knew?" Tessa just blinked at the other woman.

"Not hard to notice," Steph said. "Unless of course you're Noah."

"He's ignoring me."

"Don't let him."

"It's not that easy."

"It's not rocket science, Tessa. It's sex."

Exactly what I've been saying.

She frowned as her inner voice and Stephanie seemed to gang up on her.

Then she decided to just tell her friend what had happened last Friday. Maybe she'd planned on telling Stephanie all along. Why else would she have walked down here when a phone call would have handled it? And who better to give her a little insight than the woman who'd grown up with Noah?

"I kissed him on Friday." She said it before she could lose her nerve.

"And about time, too," Stephanie said.

Not the reaction she'd been expecting. "What are you talking about?"

"Please, Tess." Stephanie sat back in her chair and shook her head. "Just because my brother has apparently been wearing blinders for the last five years doesn't mean I have."

"Oh, God…" How embarrassing was this? How many other people in the office had noticed that Tessa was in love with the boss?

Stephanie laughed. "It's not a tragedy. So? What happened?"

"Oh, he kissed me back. I think he curled my

hair, actually," Tessa mused. "Then he left and I didn't hear from him all weekend. No business problems to handle. No plans to make."

"Unusual, I grant you," Stephanie said, nodding.

"And this morning when I saw him, he acted as if it had never happened." That still annoyed her. "He brushed it off. Said it was nothing and we wouldn't be talking about it again."

Tessa's temper began to bubble as she described that meeting with Noah. Honestly, she'd been so surprised at his attitude, she hadn't really processed how she was feeling about it.

Now that she was processing it, though, she was beyond annoyed and deeply insulted.

"Typical." Stephanie laid her forearms on her desk and leaned toward Tessa. "Well, he's lying."

"I know that. I was there. Doesn't change the situation, though." Except for making her want to charge back down the hallway, breach his office door and confront him. *Make* him admit that the kiss they'd shared was way more than he was pretending it was.

"I think it does," Stephanie said. "If it didn't mean anything, he wouldn't mind talking about it. He'd say something stupid about inappropriate behavior and be done with it." She pointed her finger at Tessa. "But him saying it doesn't mean anything and refusing to talk about it means that it *did* mean something to him and he doesn't want to think about it."

"Believe it or not, I followed that," Tessa said with a half smile. "But what does knowing it change?"

While it was great having her own thoughts on this validated, Tessa didn't know what else it did for her.

"It changes how you handle it—if you still want to," Stephanie said, then added, "and I totally understand if you just want to write him off."

"No…" The chance for writing off Noah had come and gone years ago. The day she had first realized that she was in love with her boss. With a man who would never see her as more than part of his office.

But hadn't that changed Friday night? Hadn't he, at last, really seen her? For the first time?

I told you, Tessa. Sex is the answer.

Who said anything about sex?

You should.

She shut that voice down again and focused on Stephanie.

"If you want my advice, don't let him bury it. Talk about it. The kiss, I mean. Talk about it a lot. Make him remember."

Making him remember would bring her…what? Was finally giving in to what she felt for Noah the answer? Or would it be better to just leave her job with the same hungers that had tortured her for five years?

How was she supposed to know?

"I can see you thinking," Stephanie mused aloud.

She shrugged. "Up to you, obviously. But I know my big brother. Ever since our grandfather died, Noah's been obsessed with fulfilling Papa's dream. Making Graystone the name you think of when you buy a bottle of vodka.

"It's going to take being hit over the head to sway him from that course—figuratively, of course." She grinned. "Although sometimes I consider a literal hit over the head—though I restrain myself."

Tessa laughed a little because honestly, she'd been pushed to the edge with Noah herself many times. It wasn't easy working with a driven perfectionist. Wasn't easy pretending not to care for him, either.

"Like I said," Stephanie went on, "it's up to you. But if it helps, I'm on your side."

It was good to hear, anyway. Tessa had a lot of thinking to do. Decisions to make. But meanwhile, she also had a job to do.

"It helps," Tessa said and stood up. "I don't know what I'm going to do yet—beyond get back to work, at the moment."

"Okay, well, tell Noah I'll be there in a few minutes. I just need to make a call to Marketing, get them to send me the latest report."

"I'll tell him," Tessa said and headed for the door. Stephanie was already on the phone when Tessa left the office. She took her time walking back to her desk.

Looking around the office space, she had to

admit that she would actually *miss* coming in to work every morning. Not just the people she knew and liked, but also the rush of the work itself. Helping to put Graystone on the map was exciting and now she was leaving just as Noah was within reach of the award he'd been working toward for years.

Still, she had to do this. For herself. Noah's dreams weren't hers. Tessa knew her future didn't lie here, at the company. Or with Noah. So difficult or not, she had to move on.

Now she just had to decide if she really wanted to leave and never indulge herself with Noah.

She was pretty sure she knew the answer.

"Tessa said you wanted to see me."

Noah looked up as his sister walked into the office. Stephanie was smart, capable and since taking over the position of COO had done incredible work for the company. Noah trusted her implicitly—and yet still kept up with the decisions she was making for the family business.

"Yes," he said, "since I'll be in London for a week, I thought we should talk, make sure we're on the same page."

"What page is that?" she asked, dropping elegantly into one of the visitor chairs opposite his desk. She crossed her legs, folded her hands in her lap and waited.

Patience. Steph had always had it and it worked

to her favor in negotiations with competitors and clients alike. It didn't work with Noah.

"I want to know what you're planning for when I'm out of town."

"Not a thing," she said, lifting her hands now in a show of innocence.

"Right." Shaking his head, Noah continued, "I've taken care of the meetings I need completed before I leave. The new labels designed by Ms. Shipman's company look good. I'm having her send you some mock-ups with several different colors, so you can make the final decision."

"Seriously?" Her eyebrows lifted. "Okay, good. These are labels for the varietal vodka, right?"

Their signature mix of blackberry-and-lime-infused vodka was a winner; Noah was sure of it. Once he had that award, he would focus his efforts on the pure vodka line.

"Yes, she's going to work on a different approach for the pure vodka bottles, though I think we should keep the Graystone font the same, to provide continuity to the customers. Still, I want your opinion."

"You'll have it." She smoothed the crease of her black slacks. "Tessa said you were at her house last Friday."

His head snapped up and he glared at his sister. He knew Steph and Tessa had become friends. He just didn't know if that friendship included gossip.

Hell. Of course it did.

"What else did she have to say?"

"Nothing."

He snorted. "She said nothing."

"That's right," Stephanie said with a shrug. "She said you helped her pour a couple of candles—which by the way, I would have loved to see—and that you left soon after."

"That's it."

"That's it," Stephanie repeated. "Why? Is there more?"

His frown deepened. Had Tessa really not said anything about that kiss? Or was Steph playing him? Hard to tell. Which was irritating.

"Okay then." Stephanie stood up. "If that's all, I've got a meeting with Devon in Marketing in a few minutes. He's got a couple of ideas for our next campaign that I think are brilliant."

"What are they?"

"Oh, I'll save that for when you get back from London." She headed for the door then paused and turned around. "Be sure to call me if we win."

"*When* we win, I will," he said.

"I like the attitude. You and Tessa have fun in England."

"It's business, Stephanie. It's not about fun."

She heaved a dramatic sigh. "It never is with you, is it, Noah?"

"What's that supposed to mean?" Sisters could get away with a lot more than most people, but Noah had a limit and she was cruising very close to it.

She walked back to his desk, planted both hands

on the edge and leaned down to look her brother in the eye. "It means, that you don't have to sacrifice your entire life to be the Anti-Dad."

"I'm not sacrificing anything," he countered, wondering how they'd taken this turn in the conversation.

"Sure. Noah, you might as well be a monk."

"That's ridiculous—and where is this coming from?"

"I talked to Matthew today and he's taking a couple of days in New Orleans. And I realized it's been years since you've done the same."

Noah scowled at her. "Matthew takes too many breaks."

"You think he's turning into our father or something, don't you?"

He didn't like to think it, but yeah, his younger brother had a lot of their father's less-than-great attributes. Jared Graystone had left nothing but misery in his wake, which was why Noah had done everything he could to steer his own life in the opposite direction.

Matthew had been young enough that he hadn't really been aware of the pain their father had caused. He hadn't heard their mother crying. Hadn't seen the disappointment and despair in their grandfather's eyes.

Matthew hadn't made a vow to reclaim what his father had ruined, as Noah had.

"Matt likes women, Noah," Steph said. "He likes having a life."

One eyebrow lifted. "So did Dad."

"But Matt isn't a drunk. He isn't cruel or thoughtless or any of the other things our illustrious parent was."

Noah stood up and Steph straightened to face him. "He could be, though," Noah said. "The temptations are right there and if he heads too far in the wrong direction…"

Stephanie pushed her hair behind her shoulders and sighed. "*This* is why Matt's always on the road," she said. "Yes, he's Head of Sales, but he could delegate a hell of a lot more than he does. He takes these trips to get away from your disapproval."

"Bull." Was that true?

"Noah, you're so busy worrying that Matt will become like Dad that you don't see that in the ways that matter he's *nothing* like the man. And you constantly expecting him to suddenly morph into a wastrel is exactly what's keeping him away." She shook her head. "Honestly, Noah, there's a difference between having fun from time to time, and being a complete jerk who tosses away everything that should matter."

Rationally, he knew Stephanie was right. And still he couldn't help worrying about his brother making bad decisions. Scrubbing the back of his neck, he admitted, "I don't want him staying away because of me. He does a great job here, Steph. I just…"

"Worry. Always worry." Stephanie walked around the edge of the desk and gave him a hug. When she pulled back, she said, "Maybe you could try dialing it down a little? Remember, Papa raised us, too. Not just you. And we saw how unhappy Mom was when Dad left. And how much happier she is now. Do you begrudge her that?"

"Of course not."

She smiled at him. "Good answer. Then don't get bent out of shape when Matt and I take a vacation. Or actually have sex once in a while."

Noah winced. "Yeah, I'm not talking about my little sister's sex life."

She laughed. "Fine, let's talk about yours. Or your *lack* of one."

"My sex life is none of your business." His voice was clipped, with the dismissive tone that clearly said the conversation was over. "Don't you have a meeting to get to?"

"Maybe if you *had* sex occasionally, you'd be easier to deal with."

"Butt out."

She shrugged. "Fine. But maybe you should ask yourself something. Now that Tessa doesn't work for you anymore…maybe your trip to London could be a 'break' as well as a business trip."

His eyes narrowed on her. "You said she didn't say anything to you."

Stephanie patted his cheek. "Clearly, I lied."

Five

Three days later, Noah was on edge.

Yes, he and Tessa had always worked closely together. But these days, that closeness had really become...overwhelming.

It seemed every time he turned around, she was there, leaning over his desk, brushing her hand against his as she handed him a report. Even when she buzzed his office and spoke to him, her voice sounded different. Huskier. Softer. Tempting.

Scowling, he realized that thoughts of Tessa were clouding his mind when he most needed clarity of thought. With the international spirits awards the following week, he needed to be on his game now more than ever.

Some would say that it didn't matter. The votes had been counted, the award decided. There was nothing he could do at this point. But Noah didn't believe that. Sure, the awards were sealed and would be announced in the middle of the conference. But before and after the ceremony, there were people to talk to. New links in the chain to be forged. Commitments to be made. He wanted to get Graystone Vodka around the world and to do that, he needed to make alliances with his counterparts in Europe.

Before the awards, he would be laying down the groundwork for what might come. And once his vodka had won that blasted award, he wanted to be able to move fast on distributors and marketing and every other damn thing required.

The problem was, he couldn't focus on any of it if Tessa kept filling his mind.

Which was why he was here, outside her house again. Not because he missed her, he told himself firmly. Not because he wanted another taste of her. No. This visit was strictly business. To lay down some ground rules. To remind her that this trip to London was too important to blow.

He stopped on her front walk in the darkness and looked at the would-be fairy-tale cottage. Inside was the woman who had been driving him insane for days. Was it a mistake to be alone with her outside the safety of the office? Probably. Had he *ever* been afraid of a challenge? Never.

Scowling to himself, he thought he had also

never encountered a challenge quite like Tessa, but that wasn't important right now. What was important was to get a few things straight between them so that the upcoming trip wouldn't be affected.

His long legs made short work of the cobblestone walk and when he got to the porch, he might have knocked on that heavy wooden door a bit harder than was necessary. The door swung open a moment later and there she was. A little breathless, a little harried. Her long blond hair was pulled up into a ponytail at the back of her head and she wore yet another short, clingy T-shirt—this one red. She wore skin-tight yoga pants with a red-and-green floral pattern and her toes were now painted blue. He shook his head at that, but he didn't have long to admire her.

"Oh, thank God you're here." Tessa grabbed his hand, pulled him into the house and swung the door shut with a slam behind him. Tugging him along behind her toward the kitchen, she was saying, "I need help. The overnight service will be here in a half hour and Lynn, my neighbor, had to go home because her son was sick. There's no way I'll get it all done on my own—" she glanced over her shoulder at him "—so you've just been drafted."

This was *not* going as he'd planned it. Noah had assumed that he'd have a calm, cool discussion with Tessa. Tell her that there would be nothing between them so they should both concentrate on business. His gaze dropped to the curve of her butt and he noted that the stretchy pants dipped low enough on her hips that a bit more of her lower back tattoo was visible. Not that it helped him identify what it was, but the view was intriguing.

Internally groaning, he reminded himself that Tessa's tattoo had zero to do with why he was here. "Drafted for what exactly?"

"You'll see." She entered the kitchen, dropped his hand and headed for the table on the far wall.

What he could see was…chaos. The scene in that tiny kitchen went against everything he'd ever known about Tessa. One of the things he'd always admired about her was her innate sense of organization. Hell, as he remembered it, even her stock of supplies in her garage were methodically organized. This… He shook his head, for once in his life, speechless.

The kitchen island, under a hanging pendant lamp, was brilliantly lit, which made it easy to see the candles in a dozen apothecary-style jars, three rolls of jewel-toned ribbon, stacks of empty boxes and packing material strewn across the counters, some of it falling to the hardwood floors.

"What happened in here?" He turned his head to look at Tessa, huddled over the small table.

Her ponytail swung as she looked over her shoulder at him. "I had to work late," she said with a tone of accusation, "so that made me late getting to all of this, but I've made a commitment to get these candles and earrings out tonight and like I said, I've only got a half an hour, so if you don't mind, we can chitchat later and you can help *now*."

"What do you expect me to do?" He knew nothing about her business, and sadly, it looked as though she didn't, either. *This* was what she was resigning for? She was walking away from a great job, good salary...*him*, for this kitchen table nightmare?

"I expect you to measure off sections of ribbon ten inches long, then tie bows around the necks of the labeled jars."

"Tying bows? Seriously?" He looked at her as if she'd asked him to perform surgery.

"Noah," she snarled, "I don't have time for this. Help me or get out if you can't handle it."

His eyebrows shot up.

"Can't handle tying bows? Please." Damned if he'd be sent away before he'd had that talk with her and if that meant dealing with ribbon, then he'd do it. How hard could it be?

"Fine." He took off his jacket, tossed it onto an empty space on the kitchen counter and picked up the wide red ribbon to begin. He used the ruler lying there to measure, then cut it and tied it around the neck of the jar. Looked pretty good, if a little lopsided, to him. So he moved on. While he worked, he asked, "What exactly are *you* doing?"

"Hand addressing the boxes, packing them and sealing."

"Hand addressing?" He cut a green ribbon and

repeated the bow action. "Are we cavemen? Don't you have a printer?"

"It's the personal touch, if you must know. How many jars have you done?"

"Two," he said as he finished.

"Hurry up."

His eyebrows lifted. He hadn't taken orders in a long time and he didn't care for it, but there was no time to object. He had to help Tessa finish this so they could talk. White ribbon was next. He watched her as she walked from the table to the counter to grab two more boxes and packing material. Once she had them set up, she came to pick up the two candles he'd finished.

She lifted them, stared at them wide eyed for a moment or two, then looked at him and asked, "Did you tie these with your feet?"

"Excuse me?"

"Come on, Noah…" She undid the red bow and quickly redid it, talking the whole time. "Haven't you ever wrapped a present before? No wait a minute, I know you haven't. I wrap your presents for you, don't I? Never mind. I should have known better."

He was only half listening, but he watched every move her nimble fingers made. She made it look very easy, he silently admitted, but he could replicate her moves. "Fine. Do the packing. I can do this."

She frowned and considered it.

"Damn it, Tessa, I'm the president of a multi-million-dollar company. I can handle tying bows onto candle jars."

"Fine." She huffed out a breath. "I don't have the time to be picky. Just…be better."

Well, that was insulting, but he simmered silently as he worked. He could admit, at least to himself, his redone bows looked considerably better once he imitated Tessa's moves and he was finished in a few tense minutes. "Done."

"Great, box them up. Two to a box. Use the packing materials so the jars don't crack in shipping."

"Sure you can trust me?" He thought he'd muttered that low enough, but she heard him anyway.

"No, but I'm out of options." She wielded the strapping tape like a sword in battle. She was fast, efficient and as soon as he had the candles boxed, she was sealing them shut, slapping labels on them and pushing them to one side.

They were a good team, Noah thought. Even at something as incongruous as this. Which was exactly why her resignation made no sense. She was the right hand of the president of a huge company. She was in on every decision. Every marketing meeting, and her suggestions were always considered and usually accepted. Why would she want to toss all of that aside for…this?

When the doorbell rang, her head snapped up as she bit her bottom lip. "Get the door, will you?

That'll be Travis, here to pick these up. As soon as I strap the last two boxes, we'll be done."

"Right." Shaking his head, Noah walked down the hall, opened the door and faced a tall, dark haired guy with a wide smile on his face. Slowly, that expectant smile faded.

"Who're you?"

Irritated, Noah said, "That doesn't concern you."

The man gave him a scowl designed to intimidate. It didn't work on Noah, but that didn't stop the man from trying. "Hey, I know Tessa and I've never seen you before. Where is she?"

Exasperation was quickly swallowed by outrage. What? Did he look like a serial killer or something?

"Back here, Travis!"

At Tessa's shout, the man stepped around Noah and headed for the kitchen. Naturally, Noah was right behind him. Travis certainly seemed comfortable in Tessa's home. Just how well did she know him?

Apparently very well. Noah entered the kitchen in time to see Tessa greet Travis with a big hug as she laughed and said, "My hero!"

Travis enjoyed that hug a little too long from Noah's point of view, then he stepped back, jerked a thumb at Noah and asked, "Who's the stiff?"

Stiff?

Tessa laughed, glanced at Noah and immediately tried to swallow her smile. "That's my boss, Noah Graystone."

"No way. As in Graystone Scotch?"

"That's the one," Tessa said.

Travis turned, grabbed Noah's hand and gave it a hard shake. "Good to meet you. You make my favorite drink."

Noah bit back his annoyance long enough to say, "Thank you."

"No problem." Travis turned back to Tessa and reached out to tug at a lock of her hair. "Ready to go, Tess?"

"All set." She picked up a waybill and handed it to him. "All of the addresses are there and my account number."

"Great!" He folded the paper and tucked it into the inside pocket of the dark blue jacket he wore, then picked up five of the boxes. "I'll come back for the rest."

"Don't be silly—I can help."

Noah scowled. He wanted Travis gone as quickly as possible, so he picked up five of the boxes and Tessa grabbed the last two. "We can help," he said.

"Great." Oblivious, Travis just grinned and headed for his truck, talking to Tessa the whole way. "So when are you going to come to dinner with me?"

Was he really asking her for a date while Noah was right there? Who the hell did that?

"I'm super busy right now, Travis," Tessa said, "but maybe soon."

What the hell kind of name was Travis anyway? Was he a cowboy?

"I'm going to hold you to that," the guy said and gave Tessa a wink.

Then he stopped flirting long enough to load the truck. When everything was tucked inside, he shut the loading door and locked it. "Good to meet you," he said to Noah, then looked at Tessa. "I'll see you next week?"

"Oh, no," Tessa told him. "I'm going to be out of town for a week, so I'll call when I'm home and have a delivery going out."

"Okay, and maybe when you get back from wherever, we'll get that dinner."

She ignored Noah as if he wasn't standing *right there* and said, "Maybe we will. Thanks, Travis."

"Not a problem. See you soon, Tess!"

He hopped into the delivery truck, fired up the engine and drove off, leaving Noah and Tessa alone in the suddenly silent darkness.

Then she turned to look up at Noah. "Thanks for the help. I never would have made it in time without you."

Still annoyed, Noah muttered, "Oh, I think Travis would have waited for you."

She tipped her head to one side, frowning at the tone of his voice. "Maybe he would. He's a nice guy."

"Seems to like you a lot."

Tessa laughed. "Is that a crime now?"

"Not a crime no, just…nothing."

"Uh-huh." Nodding, she said, "Well, thanks for stopping by. See you at work tomorrow."

He caught her arm as she started to leave. "I didn't come to tie ribbons, Tessa."

"Why are you here, Noah?"

"I thought I knew," he muttered and looked off down the street where the brake lights on Travis's truck were fading.

She sighed a little and he turned his attention back to her. "Noah, I'm tired. I want to go sit down with a glass of wine and order some takeout."

"Sounds good."

"That wasn't an invitation."

"That's how I'm taking it. Consider it payment for my expert ribbon tying."

She laughed again. "You expected to be paid for what you mangled?"

"All 'your hero' did was pick up the damn boxes and he got a hug out of it."

A thoughtful expression crossed her face. "Jealous?"

"Of course not," Noah snapped. He wasn't. Obviously. He didn't get jealous because he was never in the kind of relationship where he might feel territorial. So it wasn't that at all. He just didn't like how Travis had looked at Tessa. And he really hadn't liked how long that hug she'd given the man had lasted.

A soft, chill breeze slipped past them and wrapped

Tessa's scent around Noah like a ribbon of warmth. He drew it in, holding it deep in his lungs until it felt as if it were branding itself on his soul.

Which was a completely ridiculous thought.

"Jealousy has nothing to do with it," he said and hated that his voice sounded stiff, even to himself. "I didn't like the way he was looking at you."

She waved that off. "Travis is a friend."

Tessa might see it that way, Noah thought, but it wasn't reality. "That's *not* how he was looking at you."

"Why do you care?"

"I don't." It had been aggravating to watch. That was all.

"Good. So, if it doesn't bother me, it shouldn't bother *you*."

She was right. It shouldn't. And yet.

He saw her turn for the house, wrapping her arms around her middle. "I'm going in. I'm freezing out here."

Funny. He felt as if he were on fire. But he followed her into the house anyway. They still had to have that talk, though at the moment, talking was the last thing on his mind. Tessa walked directly back to the kitchen and Noah was right behind her. He liked the view.

While she gathered the detritus left in the wake of the shipping emergency, she asked, "What did you want to talk to me about, Noah?"

Good question. For a second, he blanked on it

and couldn't remember why the hell he'd come over here in the first place. His gaze was locked on the curve of her mouth and he was mesmerized. That mouth of hers. How had he never noticed before last week, that her lips were full and tempting? How had he not wanted to know what they tasted like? How had he gone the last several days without taking another taste?

Duty, he reminded himself. Duty was the reason he'd kept his distance. The reason he was here.

He shoved his hands into his pockets. "I wanted to tell you to take tomorrow off."

She blinked, clearly surprised. "Really? Take Friday off when we're leaving for London on Saturday? Are you feeling all right?"

He frowned. Was it really so strange for him to give her a day off? He supposed it was and he'd have to think about that. Later.

"Yes. I'm fine." Tortured, but fine. "I just think it's a good idea for each of us to get ready for the trip and there's no reason to be in the office. We've taken care of everything."

"Uh-huh." She pulled the elastic from her ponytail and released her hair to frame her face and fall across her shoulders.

Was it always that wavy, with a tendency to curl at the ends? Why did he want to touch it? This was not going the way he'd planned. And he realized that was what he'd thought the last time he was in Tessa's house. Apparently, his brain took a vacation the minute he entered the place. And that should tell him he was right about what he'd come to say tonight.

Duty. That one word could keep him on his path and help him avoid the very real temptation that Tessa represented.

"There's something else," he said tightly, silently amazed that he was able to squeeze any words at all past the knot in his throat.

"I thought there might be," she mused, tipping her head to one side so her hair fell like a golden waterfall. "Think I'll pour some wine for the rest of this. Do you want some?"

"Sure. Fine."

He watched as she took two glasses from a cupboard, walked to the fridge and opened it. In a few seconds, she had the cold white wine poured. She walked back to him and handed him one—her fingers brushing lightly against his. Just what she'd been doing to him all week. Tessa took a sip of the wine and sighed in pleasure, and that tiny sound shivered through him.

Then she took a deep breath and her high, full breasts rose and fell with the action. His gaze dropped briefly to enjoy the show, then he looked into her eyes and saw the gleam there. She'd noticed. Damn it.

He set his wine down untouched. Hell, his brain was already a sieve, no point in adding alcohol to the mix. "Look. Maybe it was a mistake not to talk about that kiss."

"You think so?" She bit her bottom lip, tugging at it until he felt that tug deep inside him.

"Cut it out." His voice was deep and strained.

"What do you mean?"

Her voice was all innocence and he wasn't buying it. "You know exactly what I mean."

"I really don't, Noah." She leaned against the kitchen island, hitching one hip higher than the other. Taking another sip of her wine, she then set the glass down. Shaking her hair back, she said, "Maybe you should explain it to me."

"Yeah," he ground out. "That's what I'm talking about."

She shook her head. "Still don't get it."

"Tessa, this isn't going to happen."

"Sounds dire," she said, smiling. "What isn't going to happen?"

"You. And me. Together."

There. He'd said it.

"Okay. I'll try to heal my broken heart…"

"Funny."

"I'm not trying to be funny, Noah," she said, pushing off the island to face him. "I'm trying to understand why you think, for some reason, that I'm wasting away for you."

"I didn't say that."

"Good. So what are you saying, then?"

"Fine. You want me to spell it out?" He took a step closer and instantly regretted it. She smelled like summer and her scent wound around him like a promise.

"That kiss was…good."

"Agreed," she said with a sharp nod.

"And can't be repeated."

"Okay." So reasonable. But he looked into her eyes and saw not innocence but humor and heat, tangled together.

"Said so easily, though all week you've been…"

She smiled. "I've been what, Noah?"

"Tempting," he admitted, though it cost him.

Grinning, she reached out and laid one hand on his arm. Instantly, heat slammed into him.

"Isn't that a nice thing to say?"

Figured she'd be pleased by that. "It's not a compliment."

"Like you said earlier, I'm taking it as one."

"Fine." Shaking his head, he said, "Hell. Maybe you should. I don't want you in the office tomorrow, because I think it's best if we have some time apart before we board the plane for London."

"Afraid you can't trust yourself around me?"

Yes.

"Of course not. It's just that I can't be distracted by you, Tessa," he said firmly. "I'm closer than I've ever been to putting Graystone Vodka at the top of the list of premium spirits and I'm not letting anything get in my way."

"I'm not in your way, Noah," she said simply. Tucking her hair behind her ears, she added, "I never have been. In fact, I've done everything I can to help you reach your goal. I understand what your business means to you. It's why I quit, remember? Because I feel the same way about *my* business. So I get it. I do."

"Good." His body was still tense, his heartbeat still racing as if he'd just run a marathon.

"And in a little more than a week," she added softly, "you won't have to see me at all. I'll be out of your life completely."

He didn't like the sound of that any more than he had the day she'd turned in her resignation. Yes, he wanted to avoid entanglements that could split his focus on the driving ambition that had been pushing him forward for years. But he also couldn't really imagine his everyday world without Tessa in it.

They'd worked together for so long. He trusted her as he trusted very few people. She was a part of his life and losing her wouldn't be easy. But having her as more than his assistant would be even more difficult.

"Then we understand each other." He looked down into her pale blue eyes and couldn't seem to tear his gaze away.

"I guess we do," she said softly.

"So I'll see you on the plane Saturday morning. We leave at eight."

She nodded, still keeping her gaze locked with his. "I'll be there."

"Good. And then we'll handle business and get through the week like professionals."

"Absolutely."

"And we'll forget about that kiss."

"I don't think so," she said with a tiny shake of her head that made the curls at the ends of her hair dance.

"Yeah," he admitted, "I don't think so, either."

"So," Tessa said, "what you're really saying is stay away *and* come closer."

He scrubbed one hand across his face. Noah couldn't even remember the last time his brain had been so…muddled. "Yeah. That's what it sounds like."

Hell, why was he even here? He didn't want the distraction. Couldn't afford to have his focus split.

"Noah…"

He looked into her eyes and felt himself being drawn in. Focus? Duty? Everything he'd devoted his life to was fading away until all that was left was Tessa. And the hunger clawing at his insides.

She kept her gaze locked on his as seconds ticked past, taking his resolve with them. Hell, maybe he'd known that going to her house was a bad idea. But he'd come anyway.

Tessa took a step back suddenly and he frowned. "What?"

"In the five years I've known you," she said quietly, "I've never known you to be indecisive."

"True."

"Yet now that you're here you're not sure you want to be."

Also true, but he wasn't going to admit it. Turned out he didn't have to speak because she wasn't finished.

"You know," she continued, "I had planned on seducing you."

"Is that right?" His entire body went tight and hard in response to that confession.

"Yes, but I think I've changed my mind."

"A little late for that," he mused, "since you've been doing it all week."

"Excuse me?"

Shaking his head, Noah said, "The touches of your hand. The leaning over the desk to show me a file. Smelling so damn good the scent fills my head and empties it of everything but you."

"Thank you?" It was a question, as if she didn't know whether to be insulted or flattered.

"You're welcome." Noah's gaze swept over her quickly, thoroughly, and the heat sliding through him intensified. "So saying you've changed your mind doesn't carry a lot of weight."

"Okay, say I was doing that, now I'm not." She took another step back as if for physical reassurance. "I admit I wanted you, but I don't need to want a man who doesn't want me—or at least can't make up his mind if he does or doesn't."

Couldn't blame her for that, but she was wrong if she thought he didn't want her. He'd never wanted anything more. Never spent the better part of a week thinking about one particular woman. Never had his dreams been tormenting him with possibilities.

"Well, what if he made up his mind before he came here?"

"Did he?" Her eyes went soft with an almost liquid fire.

"If he hadn't," Noah said, taking a step closer, "he wouldn't be here in the first place."

"Okay…"

Clearly she wanted more, but Noah didn't know what else he could give her. There wouldn't be promises between them. He wasn't talking about diamond rings and white picket fences. All he was thinking about were cool sheets, hot bodies and an end to the wanting.

"You were right, before. I'm not your boss anymore. You already quit."

"I did."

"So whatever happens now is just between us." One more step and he was so close to her now he could see the flare in her eyes and hear the hitch in her breath. "Like you said when you kissed me. You wanted it, at least once. Well, there's something I want. At least once."

She licked her lips and sighed a little and Noah knew that for good or bad, the die had been cast and there was no retreat. But then he never had been much for retreating. It was always about taking the next step. Advancing. Always.

"So," he asked, "seduction over?"

"Looks that way," she said and moved toward him.

That was all the invitation he needed. He swept in, wrapped his arms around her and pulled her in close. She tipped her head back and he took her mouth in a long, deep kiss that had warning bells clanging in his brain. He shut them down because he already knew the dangers and at the moment, didn't give a flying damn about them.

Six

All Noah wanted was the taste of Tessa filling him. The feel of her body pressed to his, the brush of her breath on his cheek. He wanted to slide his hands up and down her body and to finally...*finally*, see that tattoo above her butt, up close and personal.

Her arms linked behind his head and held on as she opened her mouth to him and his tongue tangled with hers. Breaths mingling, heartbeats racing in tandem, he let his hands roam up and down her body and then slid both palms beneath the waistband of those floral yoga pants. She groaned from the back of her throat when his palms cupped her butt and squeezed, pressing her to his aching dick hard enough to ease some of the tension while at the same time creating more.

Suddenly, she broke the kiss, pulled her head back and said, "Take off your jacket."

"What?" Trying to think after that kiss wasn't easy.

Her hands were already pushing at the shoulders of his jacket so he had to pull his hands free of her behind to shrug out of the damn thing. While he was at it, the necktie went next and her fingers pushed the buttons of his shirt free. She slid her hands across his chest and the soft glide of her skin against his fired him even further, and Noah wouldn't have thought that possible. He was a man on the edge. He'd never wanted any woman the way he wanted this one and if he didn't have her in the next few minutes, it was going to kill him.

Tessa slid her hands around to the small of his back, looked up at him and grinned. "Once you make a decision, you're good to go, aren't you?"

"Stop talking, Tessa." He buried his face in the curve of her neck and tasted the pulse beat at the base of her throat. It hammered against his tongue and he smiled to himself, knowing that she was as crazed as he was. Good. She'd been torturing him all week, and Noah was glad to know that seduction was a two-way street.

"I'll stop talking if you'll get busy."

He lifted his head and met her gaze. Breath came hard and fast from his lungs. "I thought I was busy."

"There's busy and then there's *busy*," she said, pushing his shirt off his shoulders to slide off and hit the floor.

"Good point." Kissing wasn't enough. Touching her wasn't enough. He needed to be inside her and it was good to know that she was feeling the same way.

Noah lifted her off her feet and she hooked her legs around his middle, locking her ankles at his back. With both hands cupping her butt, he left the tiny kitchen with long strides and muttered, "Bedroom?"

"Upstairs."

"Of course it is." He took the stairs at practically a run and turned left when she told him to. He should have guessed.

Naturally, her bedroom was in the turret room. The curved walls, the curtains across diamondpaned windows. A four-poster bed covered by a quilt in blues and greens. Paintings of forests and oceans hung on the walls. It was as fairy-tale-like as the rest of the house and it suited her, damn it.

As much as he'd always been impressed with her business abilities, he'd seen, since he'd been to her house and noticed floral pants and painted toes and candles and lotions, that she was also creative. And less…conservative than he'd always believed her to be. So a cottage completely suited her.

It took only a heartbeat of time for Noah to see the whole damn room and then dismiss everything but the bed. That was the only thing they needed. And hell, wait much longer and he wouldn't need the bed, either. He'd just back her into a wall and slam himself home, driving them both out of their minds.

He stalked to the bed and Tessa leaned down to toss the quilt aside. Good enough, he told himself and reluctantly set her on her feet. He felt the loss of her body pressed to his instantly. And he wanted that sensation back. He didn't have to wait long. In a few seconds, they were both naked and rolling across those floral sheets in a tangle of heat and desire.

Noah's mind was empty of everything but the feel of her. The sight of her. Full, beautiful breasts, curvy behind and wide, generous hips. He'd had his fill of skinny women with more bones than flesh and he much preferred Tessa's body. He couldn't seem to stop touching her, having the silk of her skin beneath his hands. She was so responsive that every stroke of his fingers drew a sigh or a groan from her throat that nearly choked Noah.

She twisted and writhed in his arms and let him see exactly what she was feeling. She held nothing back from him and Noah had never been more aroused. Her reactions fed his own until the two of them should have set the bed on fire. And then she turned the tables on him, eagerly.

Tessa's hands smoothed over his body across his chest, down past his abdomen until her long, beautiful fingers curled around his aching dick and stroked him into a frenzy of need that blinded him to everything else. Then she slowly slid her hands across his hips then up, dragging her nails against his back and he groaned tightly, leaning down to kiss her mouth hard and fast. "You're killing me, Tessa."

"Right back at you," she whispered, licking her lips again as if to remind him how much he loved that small action.

He wanted her more than his next breath and yet, there was one thing he had to do first. Smiling to himself, he released her long enough to roll her over onto her stomach so that he could finally see her tattoo.

"What're you doing?" She looked over her shoulder at him.

"Had to see the tattoo," he said, tracing the tips of his fingers along the line of delicate marks on her skin. "I've been wondering about it for days. Your T-shirts kept giving me little peeks at the edges and now I want to see the whole thing."

She went up on her elbows but stayed in place while he continued to define the design with his fingertips.

"So?" she asked. "What do you think?"

Noah thought she had a great butt, but the tattoo? "I like it."

Just above the dimples at the small of her back was a miniature, beautifully detailed line of snow-capped mountains beneath a sea of stars. It was the stardust he'd been getting peeks at and maybe in an hour or two, he'd take the time to explore it more fully.

"Tell me about it. Later." He lowered his head to her behind and traced each shooting star with his tongue until she was writhing beneath him and his own blood was pumping so hard, he felt the solid slam of his heartbeat. When he couldn't take it another moment, Noah went up on his knees, then lifted her hips until she, too, was kneeling.

And it was only *then* that he remembered he didn't have a damn condom with him. "Damn it."

"What?" Breathless, she tossed her hair back and looked over her shoulder at him again. "Why are you stopping? What's wrong?"

"Protection." He looked into her eyes and read the same desire he knew was shining in his own. "I don't have any."

"Seriously?"

He squeezed her butt and swallowed a groan of disappointment. To be this close to claiming her and have to stop was like…finally winning that vodka award then turning it down. "Believe it or not, I haven't carried condoms in my wallet since I was a hopeful sixteen."

She actually laughed. "Good thing one of us was thinking, then. Bedside table."

He reached for it, yanked the drawer open and pulled out one of the foil-wrapped packages inside.

Yeah, she was prepared. But for *who*? Travis? Had he been up in this room, rolling on this bed with Tessa? Oh, hell no. Noah pushed that thought and the accompanying images out of his mind. All that mattered right now was this moment. This woman.

Noah sheathed himself, then went up on his knees behind her. Sliding his hands up and down her spine and back to the curve of her hips, he took his time, in spite of the heat pulsing inside him. If this was truly going to be an "at least once" kind of night, then he was going to take his time and make it one to remember. Which meant, he told himself, he wanted to be able to look into her eyes when he took her.

Flipping her over onto her back, he caught the flash of surprise in her eyes and smiled. "I want to watch you. I want to see your eyes."

"I want to watch yours, too," Tessa said and lifted her legs while she opened her arms to him.

Mouth dry, breath catching, he said tightly, "It's not going to be fast." Though silently he wondered how long he could last without losing what was left of his mind.

She swallowed hard, licked her lips and nodded. "Slow is good, too."

He smiled, stretched out alongside her. She ran her fingers through his hair, her nails scraping against his skin, then down to his shoulders and across his chest where her thumbs flicked against his flat nipples and he felt that touch right down to his bones. Noah bent his head to her left breast. He took that hard nipple into his mouth and teased the nub with his tongue and teeth.

She arched her back, groaning, as she lifted herself into his mouth and Noah smiled against her skin. While he suckled her, he slid one hand down the length of her body and dipped his fingers into her hot, damp center.

Instantly, her hands clutched at his shoulder, her fingers digging into his skin as she cried out his name. Her hips rocked into his touch and he watched her open features as she fought for a release that was just out of reach. Her eyes glazed over and he loved it.

"Noah… Noah…damn it, be in me. Be in me now."

He watched her react to his touch and felt a responding fire erupt inside him. "Screw slow," he muttered and moved to kneel between her thighs.

"Oh, yeah. Slow can come later," she whispered brokenly.

Later. Yes. Because he already knew that once wouldn't be enough.

Noah grabbed her hips, slid her closer and pushed his body into hers. Instantly, her tight, hot muscles closed around him and he groaned in satisfaction. This was what he'd been needing for days. Keeping perfectly still for a long moment, Noah savored the feel of her body clenched on his, until Tessa moved impatiently and shattered that tension.

He moved then, rocking his hips against hers, setting a pace that she raced to match. She lifted her legs, hooked them over his shoulders, to pull him in deeper, tighter and still, he wanted more.

Every sigh that slipped from her lips, every hitched breath pushed him to claim more of her. He'd been thinking about nothing else for nearly a week and he gave himself up to the glory of finally having her beneath him. Of looking into her eyes as she climbed a mountain of sensation, straining for the peak.

Noah took that climb with her, staggering forward, step by step, enjoying the climb, reaching for the top. He felt her release before he read it in her eyes and an instant before she shrieked, eyes flashing as her body shattered.

Tessa's body was still trembling when Noah found his own release a few moments later. It was more than he'd ever known before. More than he'd thought it would be. That staggering climax shuddered through him and all he could do was hold on and shout as the power of it jolted through him, splintering everything that had come before.

Tessa struggled to breathe. And that voice inside her whispered, *Who needs to breathe? Let's do that again.* She was totally on board with that, but first she needed to calm her racing heart and get air into her lungs if only so she could scream out Noah's name again.

Noah. Finally, Noah.

Collapsed on top of her, he was a heavy, warm blanket that she'd longed to feel for five years. He was still inside her, their bodies linked, and she felt something stirring inside her in response. She wasn't finished. One mind-exploding orgasm would not be enough; she knew that now. Her whole theory of do-this-at-least-once with Noah was shot down. Once was beyond great. Dozens of times wouldn't be enough. She'd waited too long for this and now she wanted more.

He pushed himself up onto his elbows and looked down at her. His eyes were a dark blue that still simmered with the heat that had claimed them both only moments ago.

"Well," he said, with a half smile curving his delicious mouth, "that was…a revelation."

"Good word for it," she agreed and lifted one hand to smooth his hair back from his forehead. Then because she had to keep touching him, she let her fingers slide down the line of his face until she could cup his cheek in her palm.

He turned his face into her touch, kissed her hand and Tessa's heart melted even further. Was that just a reaction to what they'd shared? Did he feel more for her than he could admit to? And if he couldn't admit it, what good was it? What was the hold he had on her? What was she going to do when their time together was over? How would she get past loving him, when the memory of this night would be burned into her brain forever?

"Am I crushing you?" He leaned in to plant a quick kiss on her mouth that made her lick her lips in anticipation of another one.

"No," she said, sliding her hands up and down his back, loving the feel of his sculpted muscles beneath her fingers. "I'm fine."

"Okay." He moved slightly and everything inside her lit up.

She inhaled sharply and arched against him.

"Oh," she whispered, "either stay perfectly still, or move faster."

He grinned and did the latter, as she was hoping he would. While his hips moved against her, he dipped his head and suckled at her right breast. That drawing sensation moved through her and she held one hand to the back of his head to keep him right there. His lips and tongue and teeth tormented her in the most amazing way possible while he continued to move inside her, pushing her already sensitive core to reach new heights.

God, she loved a man who could multitask.

In seconds, she was panting for release again. He lifted his head and stared down into her eyes and she was mesmerized.

Her earlier soul-splitting orgasm was forgotten as she raced toward another one. She planted her feet on the mattress and rocked her hips into his as they pistoned against her, pushing his body higher and deeper inside her. She felt every stroke. Heard every one of his racing heartbeats. Felt his breath against her skin and could only cling to him as he drove the rhythm again. As he set their pace. She wanted to do more. To push *him*.

"Roll over onto your back," she said, her voice hitching with every catch of her breath.

He grinned at her and for a second, she was absolutely lost in the power of that wide smile that she saw so rarely. But then the next second came and it was hunger. Mind-numbing hunger that drove her.

When he rolled over, he took her with him and then Tessa was on top. She sat up straight, her body impaled by his. She groaned and let her head fall back, relishing the feel of him filling her. Then she took a breath, braced her hands on his broad, muscled chest and began to move. She ground her hips against him, creating an amazing friction that drove her to move more quickly. Her body's demands couldn't be ignored, so she gave in to them gladly.

His hands were at her hips when she moved, lifting up on her knees and sliding back down his length until the pace she set took them both over. She looked down into his eyes and watched his expression shift from strain to pleasure and back again. She knew what he was feeling because she was caught in its grip, too.

Lifting her hands, she cupped her own breasts as she rode him and saw the flash in his eyes as his fingers at her hips tightened. She kept their gazes locked as she took him on a ride that she controlled this time. Her breasts were sensitive and when she pulled at her own nipples, he groaned aloud.

And then the tingling sensation at her core erupted and Tessa knew her release was coming. "Come with me, Noah."

He shook his head on the pillow. "You first. Always, you first."

"Together," she insisted and dropped her hands to him. Reaching behind her, she cupped him and gently squeezed and she saw his eyes glaze over as his body began to buck. Tessa let herself join him and she screamed when the pleasure rolled up and over her, crashing down on her with a force she'd never known before.

Her entire body trembled along with his and she felt the tiny earthquakes breaking inside her. And this time, when it was over, she collapsed on top of Noah and felt his arms come around her.

What could have been hours later, but was probably no more than a few minutes, Tessa heard him say, "Okay, I'm going to need a little more time before we try that again."

She laughed and even that tiny action set up a chain reaction of anticipation buzzing through her body. "Yeah," she admitted with a sigh, "me, too."

His hands were moving over her, sliding up and down her spine, cupping her bottom, then back up, as if he were trying to map every inch of her skin.

She was good with that. Actually, while he was stroking her, she felt like purring but that might be a little much.

Finally, though, he rolled to one side, taking her with him, Their bodies separated and she sighed at the loss even as she looked up at him and smiled.

There was a lamp burning in one corner of her room, but otherwise it was dark, so there were shadows on his face and in his eyes, but that one soft glow was enough to show her that his expression was both satisfied and confused.

Braced on one elbow, he stared into her eyes and said, "Okay, we've got a few minutes. Tell me about the tattoo."

Her smile still curved her mouth as she smoothed his hair back again, loving the silky feel of it. "You know I'm from Wyoming."

He frowned, thinking about it and then nodded. "I remember."

"Well," she said, "when I moved to California, I got that tattoo to help *me* remember."

"You thought you'd forget?" There was a laugh in his voice.

"I didn't want to risk it," she said with a shrug. "I love Wyoming. The mountains, the trees, the sky when it's so blue your eyes almost hurt to look at it. I guess I wanted a piece of it with me."

"If you loved it so much, why'd you leave?" he asked, voice soft as he smoothed one hand across her breast. "You never said."

Her breath caught and she sighed a little at the caress. Hard to think when he was touching her.

"There's a story," she said, remembering what had prompted her to leave her home. Her family. Everything she'd ever known.

"We have time."

She looked up at him and saw in his eyes that he really was curious—as she was about so much of his background. Thanks to Stephanie, she knew quite a bit about how they'd grown up, but she'd never heard it from Noah. How it had affected *him*. Maybe, she told herself, if she shared something of herself, he would return the favor.

"Okay," she said, trailing her fingers along his arm and the hand that was currently cupping her left breast. "Well, my mom and dad still live on the ranch where I grew up."

A quick smile blossomed and disappeared in a blink. "You grew up a cowgirl?"

"You could say that," she mused though she'd never thought of herself that way. It was just ranch life. Riding out to check the herd, making sure all the animals were fed and working in the blistering heat and freezing cold. "My brother and sister and I worked the ranch from the time we were little. I swear we learned how to ride a horse before we could walk."

"Sounds nice."

His voice sounded almost wistful, but she took his words at face value.

"It was," she admitted, and let herself go back into her memory. "Anyway, I got engaged to a man I'd known since we were children. He was perfect, as far as I was concerned, which just proves how wrong a person can be."

His hand on her breast stilled. "What happened?"

Tessa grabbed the edge of the quilt and dragged it across her like some sort of fabric shield she could hide behind. Which was just ridiculous when she thought about it like that, so deliberately, she tossed it aside again.

"He decided, a few weeks before the wedding, that he'd rather have my best friend," she said and couldn't quite stop the wince that accompanied the words. Not that she was still hurt or even that she regretted not marrying the no-good worthless son of a—

"He cheated on you?"

"Yes." Didn't that sound pitiful? The completely clueless bride, planning a wedding with a man she thought loved her, never suspecting that he was lying to her the whole time. "That's the simple answer. I found out later, that he and my 'friend' had been having sex for six months and I was the only one in our group who didn't know."

"No one told you?"

"No one wanted to be the one to hurt me." She still wasn't sure whether to be grateful or angry. Would they have let her marry him? Probably. And what a disaster that would have been. "Well, except for my fiancé and my best friend. They didn't mind a bit."

"I'm sorry."

"You don't have to be," she insisted, meeting his gaze squarely. "It was a long time ago. They ended up getting married, and divorced a year later, so... karma. As for me, I think it worked out in the end."

"I know it did."

"Really?" She smiled up into his eyes. "Why's that?"

"Because you're here. In a bed with me in a round room in a tiny castle, of all things. If not for them, you'd be a wife in Wyoming."

"Good point." The truth was, Tessa had gotten over the betrayal and the hurt years ago. But hearing Noah say those words brought it all home how much she would have missed if not for going through that pain.

"So that's why you left?"

"Mostly," she admitted, stroking her hand across his chest and smiling to herself at his quick intake of breath. "But then, there was my brother with his wife and kids and my sister with her husband and kids and my parents looking at me and obviously wondering when I was going to find a new man and have more grandchildren for them." She sighed a little. "After a while, it got old continuously telling them to back off—in a loving way of course."

"Of course." One eyebrow lifted again and his eyes registered his surprise. "You don't want kids?"

"I didn't say that," she countered. "I'd like to have some…eventually. But it was the feeling that everyone was counting off *my* biological clock that was irritating."

He chuckled and she scowled at him. "I don't see you with any kids," she pointed out.

"And you won't," he said fervently.

"There's that decisive tone I know so well," she mused.

"I can't be a good parent *and* make Graystone the best in the world," he said simply.

"Hmm. My father used to tell us there's no such word as *can't*." She shrugged. "You just keep trying until you can."

"Right," he said. "That presumes you want to try."

"And you don't."

"No." One word. Unequivocal.

"Why?" He went quiet and still, but she'd told him her most humiliating story, so it was her turn and she wouldn't let him figuratively back away. "Is it because of your father?"

Scowling now, Noah asked, "What do you know about my father?"

"Stephanie's told me some…"

"Of course she has." He sighed and shook his head.

"But not all. So is your dad the reason you don't want kids?"

"Let's just say I learned early that if your heart's not in it, you'll make a mess of parenthood."

He was pulling back and she didn't want that, so Tessa moved into him and draped one arm across his hip as if she could hold on to him and keep the intimacy from fading. "Steph said that you took it upon yourself to be the 'man' in the family when you were just a boy."

"Steph talks too much." His scowl told her what he thought of that, too.

"So why don't you tell me?"

Noah thought about that for a moment long enough to convince Tessa that he wasn't going to say any more on the subject. Then he proved her wrong.

"You probably already know most of it. My father left. Grandfather took us and my mom in and helped raise us and he's the one I owe. Nothing I do is about my father, Tessa," he told her, and gave her butt a squeeze. "It's always about my grandfather. I owe him. I have a duty to my family and the company and I can't just set that aside. I won't."

"No one asked you to, Noah," she said softly, carefully. "But I'm betting your grandfather wouldn't have expected you to sacrifice everything in your determination to make him proud."

"We'll never know that, will we?" Shaking his head, he pulled away from her and stood up. Then changing the subject he asked, "Where's the bathroom?"

She pointed. "In the hall. We passed it on the way here."

"Be right back." She watched him go and admired the view of his naked butt and long, muscled legs. He might seem as though he was always working, but clearly, Noah found time for working out, too.

She lay down, stared at the ceiling and sighed. Hearing him talk about his father, his grandfather, Tessa began to get a picture of why Noah was so driven. Stephanie had laid it all out so dryly, it had been almost easy to dismiss. But hearing the strain in Noah's voice as he recapped his life in a few short sentences had told Tessa just how important his duty was to him.

And she didn't see a way to change it. His grandfather was dead, so the old man couldn't give Noah permission to live a life. And until Noah finally put Graystone Vodka at the top of the market, he would never give himself the freedom to have more in his life than the company.

This night was becoming everything she'd ever dreamed of. Noah was an amazing lover and beyond sharing his body, he was also sharing something of himself. But at the same time, she felt as if this was nothing more than a very long goodbye.

Noah was perfectly clear about devoting his life to the company. And just because he wanted her didn't mean he loved her. Or needed her. It seemed he felt as if he didn't *need* anyone or anything, but success.

A few minutes later, he was standing in the open doorway, one shoulder braced against the jamb, his arms crossed over his chest. He looked like a sculpture. One created by an especially talented master. And then one corner of his mouth lifted and something inside her stirred in response.

"You look amazing," he said, "laid out across the bed, naked and waiting."

Maybe he didn't need her. But obviously, she thought, as her gaze drifted down that amazing body of his, he *wanted* her.

Tessa let go of the wishful part of her—that stubborn part that hoped for more from him—and became the woman who had agreed to a night with him. *Take what you can get, Tessa*, that voice insisted and maybe she had a point.

Lifting her arms high over her head, she stretched languorously. "I was just thinking something similar about you," she admitted.

"Well, then," he said, "are we done waiting?"

Whatever her thoughts had been moments ago, all she could think of now was Noah. "I think we are."

"We agree again," he said, pushing away from the wall and heading toward her with determined strides. "I've always said we make a good team."

And then he showed her just how good they were.

Seven

A couple of hours later, they were picnicking in Tessa's bed. Naked, with only the quilt pulled across their laps, they dug into Chinese takeout and sipped ice-cold white wine.

Halfway through the Kung Pao chicken, though, Noah thought they should talk about a few things. After all, he'd had a plan when he came over here— in spite of the fact that he hadn't stuck to it. Although, in his defense, he thought, how the hell could he keep from touching her when she looked so damn good?

Glancing at her now, with her tumbled hair and bare breasts, he felt his resolve weaken again as it had pretty much all night. It had probably been a huge mistake to go to bed with her, but he could hardly bemoan that when all he could think of was sex with her again. She got to him as no other woman ever had. He'd come here to reinforce the idea of staying away from her and had instead spent the night having the best sex of his life. Before that all started up again—and damned if he didn't want it to—it was time for reality to be reckoned with.

"What's causing the frown?" Tessa asked. "Already regretting tonight?"

Did she know him that well?

"No," he said, because no matter what, he wouldn't regret what had happened between them. "But—"

She took a sip of wine and swung her hair back behind her shoulders. "I knew there was a *but*."

He gave her a half smile. He'd talked more, laughed more with Tessa than he had with any other woman he'd ever known. Even *during* sex, the laughter and talking hadn't stopped and that was new for him, too. Usually sex was just a physical need that he was looking to satisfy. He didn't form relationships, didn't want to chat or laugh or connect in any way with whatever woman happened to be in his bed.

Tessa was different. And he wasn't sure how to react to that.

"The *but* is, that this—between us—it's not going anywhere, Tessa."

She sipped at her wine again, tipped her head

to one side and asked, "Are you trying to let me down easily?"

When she said it like that, it sounded stupid. "I just don't want you making more of this than there is."

"Well, thank you," she said and picked up a piece of chicken. She popped it into her mouth, then sucked at her finger to get the sauce off.

Watching that made Noah's dick go to stone—as it had been for most of the night. Taking a breath, he said, "I only meant that we were doing the 'just once' thing and now that's done."

"And more than once," she pointed out.

"Yeah, that's true. But we need some ground rules now, before we go to London."

"Okay," she said, the soul of reason, "what did you have in mind?"

Well, that was the question, wasn't it? What he wanted, was Tessa. Again. What he didn't want, were messy complications. So he took the honesty route and told her exactly that.

"Messy," she mused with a sip of her wine. "As in, me clinging to your manly self, begging you to love me?"

His gaze narrowed on her. Hearing her say it out loud sounded extremely stupid. "No. That's not what I meant."

"Okay, then what?"

"Tessa, this isn't going to be anything more than it is."

"Noah, you already said that. And if you think I wasn't aware of it before tonight, you're wrong."

That surprised him. "Is that right?"

"Oh, Noah." She waved one hand, smiled and shook her head. "For five years, I've watched you sidestep any woman who wanted more than a night or two with you. I've bought your 'goodbye' gifts to the women who got too close." She sighed a little. "You avoid relationships like they're garlic and you're a vampire."

He snorted. "Thanks."

"I'm just saying, I'm a big girl and I'm not asking you for anything—" she pointed to a carton near his thigh "—except more fried rice."

He handed it to her and watched as she put some on her plate. She seemed fine. Not all soft and gooey. But somehow, hearing her dismiss him stung more than he'd thought it would. He was accustomed to giving the "no expectations" speech. He was not accustomed to having that speech brushed aside as if it didn't matter in the slightest.

After a few seconds of silence, she huffed out a breath, glanced at him and said, "You're looking at me weird."

"No, I'm not. I just didn't expect you to be—"

"Realistic? Pragmatic?" She sat up straight, lifted her chin and added, "Eminently reasonable?"

"Yeah," he said. "All of the above."

"Great. I love being surprising."

"Of course you do." Shaking his head, he reached for the beef and broccoli and took a bite.

"Honestly, Noah, don't worry about it." She reached out and laid one hand on his thigh. "Remember, this was just a onetime thing."

He laughed at that and had a sip of wine. "A one-time thing that turned into how many?"

"Okay," she said, still smiling, "then a one-*night* thing."

"Right. And that's okay with you?"

"Sure."

Well, it wasn't all right with him. He didn't want a lifetime with Tessa or anything, but he damn sure wanted more than one night. He wasn't going to get it, but it would have been nice if she'd been a little more…upset about the situation. And even as he thought it, Noah knew he was being ridiculous. Didn't change anything, though.

"So we put tonight behind us, go to London and take care of business." It wasn't a question, but he still waited to see what she would say about it.

"Well, we could," she said, licking her fork now, forcing Noah to watch her tongue flick at the tines. He just managed to stifle a groan.

Forcing his concentration back to what she was saying—not doing, he said, "We could. Or…?"

"Or," she said, looking at him with a small smile tugging at one corner of her mouth. "We could take the time in London to…enjoy each other before we go our separate ways."

"Enjoy each other." He stared into her eyes and told himself that had to be the best suggestion he'd heard in a very long time. Maybe it wasn't the smartest thing to do, but damned if it didn't *feel* right.

"Why not?" She shrugged and her magnificent breasts moved with the action.

Noah knew that he should probably get up and get dressed and leave now. He was usually a one-night-and-goodbye kind of man. More than one night risked connections, emotions from women who always wanted more from him than he was willing to give.

But leaving right now wasn't even on his radar. A week with Tessa in his bed sounded too good to pass up. Hell, he had nothing to lose here. Besides, Tessa was being extremely reasonable. She knew this wasn't going anywhere. Knew he didn't do relationships. All they were talking about was sharing six amazing nights before they said goodbye.

"If I haven't told you this often enough," Noah said, "let me say, you're a brilliant woman."

"I'm glad you think so," she said, smiling. "And I agree. More wine?"

Friday night snacks was at her house this week and Tessa went all out. For her. She was never going to put out a spread as nice as Lynn's, but neither would they starve.

Sliced bell peppers and ranch dip, salami and cheddar on crackers, popcorn and plenty of wine.

For the kids, she'd pulled up a movie on Netflix and plied them with ice cream.

"This is really good," Carol said, reaching for another salami cracker.

Lynn just looked at her. "Have vegetables, too. What kind of doctor are you anyway?"

"A hungry one." Carol bit into the cracker and salami then grinned.

The kitchen was warm and cozy, the rumble of laughter rolled in from the living room and Tessa was there with her friends. She sighed happily and listened to Carol and Lynn argue the merits of meat versus veggies. Meat was winning.

Tessa grabbed a red pepper and dipped it before taking a big bite. Shrugging, she looked at Carol. "It's actually pretty good."

"Fine." She took one just to please Lynn, took a bite and looked at Tessa. "So, interesting thing… we saw Noah's car in your driveway last night."

"Is that right?" Tessa poured them all some more wine.

"Carol, you said you wouldn't tease her."

"Much," she corrected her wife. "I said I wouldn't tease her *much*."

Lynn rolled her eyes and looked at Tessa. "Sorry about her."

Tessa laughed. "It's okay—yes, Dr. Nosey, he was here last night."

Thoughtfully, Carol tapped one finger to her chin. "Pretty late, too…"

Still laughing, Tessa asked, "Were you clocking him?"

"No," Carol said in an unconvincing protest.

"Yes," Lynn corrected. "Okay yes, we kept tabs on him. We were...worried."

"We were nosey," Carol admitted and snatched another cracker with salami and cheese. "So what happened?"

"You know what happened," Tessa countered with a quick look down the hall to make sure the kids were still in the living room. She didn't want to end up giving a surprise sex-ed course.

"Come on, honey. Control yourself," Lynn said, shaking her head. Carol only looked at her wryly in challenge until Lynn confessed, "Fine. I'm as curious as she is. I admit it."

"Hah. Vindication," Carol muttered and toasted Tessa with a glass held high.

Lynn kept talking. "I was feeling so bad about having to leave you with all of the packages to wrap up and address, but Evan was sick—"

"As the doctor in the family," Carol tossed in, "I'm going to say it was chocolate-chip syndrome. Lynn found the empty bag in the back of the pantry. Apparently, our son decided he needed chocolate and ate them all."

"Yes, well it seemed like the flu at the time." Lynn frowned at Carol, "I was working in my office on the new earrings when he did it and—"

"Not your fault, Lynn. Our son's love of sugar

is legendary." Carol sighed. "I should have been a dentist."

Lynn laughed, then looked back at Tessa. "Anyway, while I was taking care of him, I glanced out the window and saw Noah arrive."

"And never saw him leave…" Carol's eyebrows lifted high on her forehead. "So how was he?"

Now that she could finally get a word in, Tessa said on a sigh, "Amazing."

"Oh," Lynn sighed, too. "That's wonderful. Worth waiting for then?"

"Big time."

"And?" Carol asked.

"And what? There is no more." Tessa shrugged and kept a blank expression on her face. She didn't want her friends to worry about her and even more than that, she didn't want to hear any protect-your-heart speeches. She knew what she was doing. Probably.

Sex, Tessa. Great sex.

That was true enough, but it was so hard to keep the words *I love you* from spilling out when Noah touched her. And if she did that, it would be the end. Well, she wasn't ready for it to end. Not yet.

Continuing, she added, "We shared amazing sex, very little sleep and I had today off to get ready for the London trip."

"Uh-huh." Lynn took a pepper, bit into it, then waved what was left of it to make her point. "He didn't say anything about—you know, more than one night?"

"He did." In fact, Tessa squirmed a little in her chair as she remembered the discussion they'd had after deciding to be together while they were in London. "We're going to enjoy ourselves in England and then we're done."

"And you're okay with that?" Lynn looked worried.

So was Tessa, but she wasn't going to admit it. "It's an extra week with him, so yeah, I am."

It would be devastating later, but she would deal with the pain if it meant she could have him to herself for just a little longer.

"And you're going to be cool with walking away at the end of the week?" Carol didn't look convinced.

"*Cool* isn't the word I'd use, but I will walk away." She lifted her chin. "I have to."

"Oh, sweetie…" Lynn reached out and squeezed Tessa's hand. "That's going to be so hard for you."

It was going to be really ugly and Tessa knew it. She accepted it. But she was willing to pay the price. Love made you stupid, she thought, and wished, not for the first time, that she weren't so nuts about a man who couldn't have been less interested in love.

"She'll make it." Carol nodded sharply. "I think you're doing exactly the right thing, Tess. Use him then lose him."

Tessa laughed sharply.

"Carol!" Lynn just stared at her.

"Well, come on, honey," Carol said. "Tess has been in love with this guy for freaking ever. She can get her fill of him in five or six days and then move the hell on."

"Right. Would it be so easy for you to walk away from me?"

"Come on, you guys…" Tessa looked from one woman to the other.

"Of course not, honey," Carol said. "I love you."

"Just like Tessa loves Noah, though he probably doesn't deserve it, if he can't see how wonderful she is."

"See there?" Carol grinned. "We agree! Tessa, do what you have to do. We'll be here when you get home."

She looked at her friends and smiled. From the living room came Jade's and Evan's laughter. No matter what happened after England, Tessa told herself, she'd be all right. It might take a while, but she'd live through it. She had a life to build, a business to work on and friends she could count on.

For six nights of seduction with Noah, Tessa was willing to risk the pain.

Flying private was really the only way to travel, Noah told himself. The company jet was sleek and comfortable and flew on *his* timetable, not the airlines'.

They'd get into London early evening and go straight to the Barrington. He'd already arranged with the hotel to have dinner and champagne waiting when he and Tessa arrived and then he had other plans. Plans that had been building in his mind since leaving Tessa Thursday night.

He shifted a look at her now and felt his blood buzz. Her hair was pulled up and back from her face, but she wasn't wearing her usual uniform of conservative suit and sensible heels.

Instead, she wore a red, off-the-shoulder blouse tucked into a short black skirt and mile-high red heels. Had she chosen the outfit just to drive him nuts on the hours-long flight? If so, she'd succeeded. She was tapping diligently on her iPad, getting some work done while she relaxed on the brown leather sofa. She wasn't paying attention to him. Wasn't deliberately trying to be seductive. And yet…he was practically salivating as he watched her.

Amazing how a man's view could change so completely. For five years, he'd worked with Tessa and had only occasionally acknowledged that she was an attractive woman.

Now he looked at her and felt his heartbeat thump, his blood quicken and his body go tight and hard. One week with Tessa stretched out in front of him and Noah was determined to relish every moment of it. Yes, there was plenty of work to do during the week and she would help him with that, as she always had. But at this conference, there would be so much more between them.

"You're watching me," she said and never looked up from her tablet.

He grinned. "How do you know?"

"I can feel it."

"Nice to know I'm so powerful," he mused and stood up to walk over to her. Taking a seat on the couch himself, he glanced at the iPad. "You're looking at dogs?" Surprised, he added, "I thought you were working."

She glanced at him. "I was, and when I finished, I went to the website of the animal shelter near my house."

"Okay," Noah said, watching her scroll through the faces of dogs from Great Danes to Yorkies. "Window shopping?"

She gave him a quick smile. "In a way. I'm going to get a dog. I've wanted one since I moved to California. And I don't want to buy some special puppy, either," she said firmly, "I want to get a rescue from the shelter. Find a dog who needs me as much as I need her—or him. I don't care if it's a girl or a boy."

"Why didn't you get one before?"

She turned to look at him and her hair slid across her shoulder in a thick blond rope. "Because I was never home, Noah. It wouldn't have been fair to the dog to be left alone all the time."

He felt a little stab of guilt even though it made no sense. He'd given her a great job with excellent pay and benefits and now he was supposed to feel bad about her not being able to have a pet?

As if she knew what he was thinking, Tessa said, "It's not your fault, Noah. Lots of people keep pets even though they work too much. But I couldn't do it. Anyway, none of that matters now, because now I can have one."

Because she wouldn't be working for him anymore. Because after this week, he wouldn't see her again. Funny. That thought was more depressing than he would have thought it would be. She wanted a dog. She wanted time to work on her own business. Maybe she could have all of that. Maybe, Noah told himself, he could come up with an offer that would keep her with him at work—even if the affair would have to end.

He frowned thoughtfully. But would it have to end? After all, an adult, sexual relationship didn't have to be bogged down by hearts and flowers and expectations of love and forever. They were *great* together, so why should they stop? Hell, it was actually a perfect arrangement. He smiled to himself as he considered things from all angles.

Tessa had already admitted that she knew he didn't want a relationship. She wasn't looking for one, either, so why shouldn't they enjoy the sexual bombshell they created together? With no promises given on either side, they were simply adults enjoying themselves.

So instead he thought about finding a way to

keep Tessa at work and make sure she had what she was so convinced she needed.

"What kind of dog are you looking for?"

"Growing up, I had a black Lab, so that would be perfect," she said, scrolling past hopeful, furry faces. "Oh, look at that cutie. But honestly, it doesn't matter to me. I just want a dog to keep me company while I work from home."

He frowned again. A dog to keep her company sounded better to her than working with him. Well, he wasn't going to give up so easily. He was going to come up with the perfect compromise and use their week in England to convince her to stay on with the company. With him. They could find a way around their sexual relationship and still work together. Why the hell should he lose the best assistant he'd ever had just because they were great in bed together?

And Tessa would see that it made more sense to stay at her job than to risk everything on a from-home business that might or might not ever support her. Hell, get the dog, he thought. Noah would make sure she was home enough to ease her conscience.

He smiled to himself and when she caught him, she asked, "What're you thinking?"

"I'm thinking," he lied smoothly, "that it's time to relax before we start the next frantic week."

"I am," she said and pointed to the tablet. "Dogs."

"Yeah, I've got a better idea, Tessa." He took the iPad from her and tossed it to the end of the sofa.

"Hey…"

He pressed a button along the wall and Hannah, his flight attendant, appeared from the cockpit. "Yes, sir?"

"We're ready, Hannah. Can you set it up?"

She smiled. "Of course."

"What are you up to?" Tessa asked warily.

"You'll see." A few moments later, Hannah was back, carrying a tray holding a bowl of popcorn and two iced glasses of soda. "Thanks, Hannah, you can start when you're ready."

"Yes, sir. If you need anything else, I'll be up front with the pilots. Just buzz me."

"Fine."

"What's going on, Noah?" Tessa accepted one of the glasses and took a sip.

"You'll see."

A moment later, the jet's window shades slid smoothly down, the lights dimmed and a wide screen dropped from the ceiling at the front of the plane.

"A movie?" she asked, turning to smile at him.

"Why not?" He dropped one arm around her shoulder as the movie opened. "We'll eat some popcorn and have a good old-fashioned make-out session."

She leaned closer and gave him a quick kiss. "That sounds great."

When she turned her head to watch the screen, Noah watched her. And he ignored the twinge of something unexpected squeezing his heart.

Eight

The Barrington was everything a five-star hotel should be.

Bordering beautiful Hyde Park, the Mayfair district boasted elegant Georgian homes, exclusive hotels and a wide selection of gourmet restaurants. And the Barrington, in Tessa's opinion, was the crown jewel. It was dignified and stylish, with a gray stone facade, and two uniformed doormen patrolling the entrance in bright red topcoats and black caps.

The interior was just as impressive, with gleaming tile floors, ruby-and-emerald rugs and scarlet couches and chairs set up in conversational groups. Of course, Tessa knew that by Sunday, there would be more chairs, more sofas dotting the lobby, to accommodate the two thousand people attending the spirits conference and awards. But for now, the hush of the luxurious hotel only added to the exclusive feel that surrounded them.

When they checked in, Noah and Tessa were whisked to the private elevator that took them to a penthouse suite. And now, while Noah was on the phone, Tessa explored their suite, admiring it all.

Polished hardwood floors with beautiful rugs in muted tones. Wide windows and a set of French doors in the living room and the master bedroom that opened onto a long balcony that provided a view of London that took her breath away.

There was a dining room with elegant Georgian-style furniture, and the main room boasted three overstuffed sofas, several tables and lamps that looked, and probably were, antique. A gas fireplace with red tile accents was cold and quiet now and the wide-screen TV hanging above it was dark.

She looked toward the hall that led to the bedrooms and felt her heartbeat quicken. There were two bedrooms, but they'd only be using one. Tessa's insides sparkled with expectancy and she squashed it momentarily. She had to start getting a grip on her feelings. She was in so deep now that she knew the pain of leaving Noah was going to be tremendous. If only she were able to keep love out of the equation. But then, if that were possible, she wouldn't be in this situation at all, because she'd have stopped loving him years ago.

She threw a quick look at him when she recognized the friendly but cool tone he was using on the phone, and knew he was talking to a potential business partner. Probably someone who had also arrived early for the conference.

"That's very good news, Henry," Noah was saying as he walked toward her and drew his fingertips along the length of her arm. Tessa shivered. He gave her a smile while he listened to Henry, then said, "I'll have my sister call the lawyers. We can leave our legal team and yours to hammer out the details."

Tessa smiled to herself. Henry… Had to be Henry Davenport of Davenport Freight, operating out of Birmingham. She knew that Graystone and Davenport had been doing some negotiations for nearly a month, but it seemed as if they'd reached a compromise. Barely an hour in England and he'd already sealed at least one deal. Noah Graystone was, if nothing else, a formidable businessman.

But then, Tessa had known that for years.

She opened the French doors and stepped out onto the balcony. There were huge terra-cotta pots every five feet, boasting actual trees that were bare now for winter, but at their bases were a few of the last winter flowers bravely blooming in spite of the cold.

The iron railing seemed sturdy, but since they were so high up, she didn't test it by leaning. Still,

Tessa let her gaze sweep across the spread of London as lights jumped into life. The sky was clear, the wind was icy and in the room behind her was her lover.

She folded her arms across her middle and hugged that thought to her. Noah Graystone was her lover. It was temporary, yes, but no less real.

"Aren't you freezing?" Noah came up behind her and wrapped his arms around her.

Every trace of cold disappeared instantly as heat swamped her. "I was." She tipped her head back to smile up at him. "Now I'm not."

He held her tighter. "Are you tired? It was a long flight."

"Not at all." Flying in Noah's private jet was a lot less exhausting than flying commercial.

"Glad to hear it," he said, and turned her in his arms so he could kiss her.

And even if she'd been asleep on her feet, that kiss would have woken her up completely. He lifted his hands to cup her face, holding her still for a kiss that opened up every cell in her body and sent that voice inside her to singing an abbreviated "'Hallelujah' Chorus."

She could have stood there with him forever, but there was a knock at the door and he lifted his head, took her hand and said, "Come on. That'll be dinner."

Her knees were a little shaky, but when he tugged

her along behind him, she followed. "When did you have time to order?"

"Yesterday," he said with a wink. "Made a few calls. Set a few plans into place."

"Is that right?" Tessa's smile blossomed. "Anything I should know about? I mean, I am your assistant. I should probably be kept up to speed on your plans."

"Oh, you're intimately involved," he assured her and gave her a wide grin. "Be right back."

The full force of that smile was really tremendous. She saw it so rarely—though more in the last week than in the last five years—that it still took her breath away.

He opened the door to room service. A man in a tuxedo jacket pushed in a soundless cart with a crisp, white tablecloth covering it. On the cart were dishes beneath silver domes, heavy flatware, crystal flutes and scarlet napkins. Another man followed the first, carrying an ice bucket and a bottle of champagne.

Noah signed the tab, thanked the men and saw them out.

"What's for dinner?" Tessa walked to the cart and lifted one of the heavy domes. Instantly, the scent of pasta and steak lifted into the air and she was suddenly hungry. "That smells amazing."

"But first, some champagne. Nothing wrong with toasting to a good week, is there?"

She set the dome back in place. "Not at all."

He poured for them both, then handed her one of the crystal flutes. He tapped the lip of his to hers and the chime seemed to ring out in the quiet room. She took a sip to ease the sudden dryness in her throat.

As she did, Tessa tried to figure out what Noah was up to. Yes, they'd agreed to having a week-long affair, but why was he being so over-the-top seductive? First the movie and make-out session on the jet. Now champagne in a penthouse? He didn't have to work this hard at seducing her so why was he?

Was it possible that he'd realized he *cared*?

"No thinking," Noah said as if he could see the wheels in her brain turning.

"Okay. No thinking." It was almost impossible to keep her mind straight around Noah anyway. There would be plenty of time later to try to decipher what was going on with him.

He moved in on her to plant a kiss on her mouth. If he was trying to make her stop thinking, he was doing a great job of it. Tessa dove into that kiss, letting everything but the moment fade away. This was what she'd waited for, dreamed of, for five years. Why would she waste a second of it?

When his phone rang, he lifted his head and she slanted a quick look at it. "No thinking. And no phone?"

"Definitely no phone," he agreed and left her long enough to walk over, pick up his phone and turn it off. "I've already left a do-not-disturb order at the desk, so the hotel phone won't be ringing, either."

Okay, something was definitely up, Tessa thought, as her heart raced. The man never turned off his phone. The fact that he was doing it tonight had to mean something. The question was…*what?*

He walked back to her and Tessa didn't need another sip of champagne to make her blood bubble. The look in his eyes was enough to do it.

"Dinner now?" he asked, setting his glass down. "Or later?"

Staring up into those dark blue eyes, Tessa set her flute down beside his. "Later," she said, telling herself it didn't matter right now what his motivation was. She'd already decided to revel in the time they had together. The future could take care of itself. She was more interested in the present. "Definitely later."

"Good choice."

He swept her up into his arms and stalked toward the master bedroom. The bed had been turned back already and she barely had a moment to enjoy the huge room with its luxurious appointments.

The bed was gigantic and covered in a burgundy comforter. Bright white sheets stood in stark contrast to the darkness of the duvet. A mountain of pillows was stacked against the headboard and one of the bedside lamps was turned on, its low light spilling across the mattress in invitation.

Noah set her down and hurriedly undressed. She watched him as she did the same, each of them tossing their clothes to land all across the floor and the chairs drawn up near a small, tiled fireplace on one wall.

When they were naked, Tessa took a moment to enjoy what a picture he made. Then he gave her a slow smile that lit off fireworks inside her.

"I didn't just order dinner. This time, I'm prepared," he said and pulled the bedside drawer open. When he pulled out two boxes of condoms, Tessa grinned.

"I like preparation. It's very sexy."

"Damn straight," he said, taking one of the condoms before dropping the boxes back into the drawer.

She watched him slide the latex on and thought about what he'd done. Two boxes. He was planning a busy week. And Tessa was all for it.

When he was ready, he came to her, gave her a gentle push that had her tipping over onto the bed. Her laughter died though when he reached down and flipped her over onto her stomach. Instantly, her mouth went dry and her body quivered.

Her hard nipples scraped against the duvet, cool against her skin, and sent sensation shooting through her. Taking a breath, she looked back at him and saw his eyes burning with desire as he scraped his hands up and down her back and onto her butt. He squeezed her flesh hard and she gasped with pleasure. Then he stroked her core with his fingertips and in an instant, Tessa's body was coiled and waiting.

He grabbed her hips and hitched her up higher. Tessa went up on her knees, eager now for what was coming.

He bent low to kiss her tattoo and she was never so glad as then that she'd had it done. It seemed to fascinate him and Tessa loved knowing that.

"Higher, Tessa," he whispered.

She lifted her hips higher and rested her head on her forearms, braced on the bed. He pushed himself deep inside her and she sighed as she took him all the way in. Her body trembled with every stroke. Tessa groaned aloud when she couldn't hold it back any longer and clenched her fingers into the silk duvet beneath her.

She moved back into him, helping him claim her. Taking him as deeply as she could while she matched the hard, fast pace that Noah set for them. Electricity seemed to buzz all around the room, where the only sound was strained breaths and the muffled groans that erupted from their throats.

Tessa had never needed so much or felt so much or wanted so much. To have Noah inside her was everything. To hear his breath rushing from his lungs, to feel his hands at her hips, holding her to him, was more than she'd ever imagined. Every time with him was better than the last time. They were linked. Whether he could see it or not, that connection between them was real and strong.

And it deserved more than a week.

"Come on, Tessa. Come. Let yourself go and come." His words were ground out as if it had been a personal victory to be able to speak at all. And maybe it had been.

Tessa didn't think she could have formed words at all.

Then her mind emptied as she raced toward that next release. She fought for breath, felt her heart pounding in her chest, the tingling sensation rising up from deep inside her. She bit her lip and tightened her grip on the cool silk of the duvet. Again and again, he pushed her, silently demanding she give him all she was. Refusing to accept less. And finally, she did. There was no stopping it. No prolonging it.

She screamed into the bed, hoping the mattress would muffle the sound, and pushed her body back against him in one frantic last jump into oblivion.

Moments later, he held her tighter, ground himself against her and shouted her name like a warrior's triumphant call after a battle.

When he collapsed onto the bed, he wordlessly rolled over and drew her with him, tucking her into the circle of his arms. Tessa laid her head on his chest, draped one leg over his and smiled as she listened to the hard beat of his heart.

She loved him. She always would.

And the heartbreak was, she couldn't tell him.

* * *

The Aston Martin Noah had requested was delivered to the hotel and on Sunday, their first full day in England, they went for a ride. A long one, as it turned out, since Tessa had mentioned that she'd always wanted to see Stonehenge. Noah had instantly jumped into action. Salisbury was almost two hours from London and they probably should have simply taken the train. But nothing was going to stop Noah from driving that car.

Early December in England was cold and damp, so they were dressed for it in jeans and jackets, and they'd brought a couple of umbrellas with them. Still, the weather didn't dissuade people from making the trip from London. There were a lot of tourists at the site and Tessa guessed that a good number of them were in London for the conference.

"Does it meet expectations?" he asked, staring at the ancient standing stones ten yards from them.

"Oh, yes," she said. "I wish we could get closer, but this is wonderful."

He held the umbrella over both of them to keep off the soft, steady rain. "If I'd known you were interested, I'd have arranged a private visit in advance."

Tessa looked up at him. "Oh, thanks, but this is great." Shifting her gaze back to the massive stones, she shook her head and said quietly, "Can you even imagine what it took for people to set these stones in place?"

"Is this another lesson in 'there's-no-such-word-as-can't'?"

She glanced at him and saw him smile. "Let's just say my dad would approve of those people's determination." Turning her gaze back to the stones, she sighed a little. "You can almost feel the magic, can't you?"

He was looking at her when he said, "Yeah. I suppose so."

"You're watching me again."

"I like the view."

She turned to face him and the cold wind racing across the open ground lifted her hair and threw it across her eyes. She plucked it free and said, "Thanks for bringing me here, Noah. I've always wanted to see it."

He frowned a little. "You should have said something last summer when we were in London."

"We were working every minute," she reminded him.

"We could have taken one afternoon," he argued.

"Really?" She gave him a wry smile. Because they both knew that would never have happened. Noah's focus was on the company and everything else in the world simply didn't exist for him. She hated knowing that he was deliberately missing out on so much, but she'd never been able to make him see the truth.

"Okay, I probably wouldn't have," he admitted. Shifting his gaze to the stones where ancient people had once lived and prayed and died, he added, "I should have, though."

"You're here now," she said, and leaned her head against his shoulder. "That's enough."

Rain pattered against the umbrella and the mist lay heavily across the open land surrounding the stones. Magic seemed to pulse in the air and for a moment, when Noah took her hand and folded his fingers around hers, Tessa felt that magic deep in her bones.

Noah's first meeting on Monday went even better than expected.

He left the dining room, satisfied with the progress of his negotiations with Billingsley Bottling. Charles Billingsley was eager to grow his company and taking it international was a huge part of that. Noah wanted a bottling plant in the UK, to help sales grow and to meet the rising demand they were already experiencing. He'd call Stephanie to let her know so she could run backup and nail this down, hopefully this week.

He hadn't seen Tessa in several hours and silently, Noah told himself that was probably a good thing. After their excursion to Stonehenge, it felt as if something had changed between them. Rather than just the heat of desire, he'd been feeling something…deeper. Richer. And he wasn't sure what to do about that.

Sex was one thing.

Relationships were another.

He'd begun to rethink his idea of somehow getting her to stay at the company. Especially if they continued this affair. If what was between them became messy and involved, then that would be too big a distraction. He couldn't afford that. He had a business to grow. He had neither the time nor the inclination to build anything else.

No, the only way to keep Tessa at the company was to end the affair and try to wipe his memory of the times spent with her. Not easy, of course, but necessary.

With that thought in mind, he caught a glimpse of Tessa, across the lobby. She wore a deep blue blouse with a high collar and long sleeves along with that short black skirt she'd worn on the plane and a pair of black stilettos that somehow made her long legs look even longer. She stood out in this crowd of stolid, conventional people and he wasn't surprised to see heads turn as people passed her. Noah frowned, though, as he watched a tall man walk up to Tessa, shake her hand and give her a smile designed to charm.

Of course, he recognized the man as Marcus Campbell of Campbell Bottling, out of Glasgow. The man took Tessa's hand between both of his and held it for longer than necessary, then leaned in and said something to make Tessa laugh. Noah's scowl deepened as he wondered what the two of them were laughing about. And why did Tessa look so pleased to see Marcus Campbell?

Noah had seen her with competitors and allies alike over the last five years and he'd long ago acknowledged that she'd always had the ability to smooth things over, or to make inroads with people who were of interest to Graystone. But he'd never seen her smile like that before. Or maybe he'd never noticed. Hard to believe but it was a possibility, because until the last week and more, Noah had never treated Tessa like a "woman." She was his assistant. Someone he depended on.

No doubt she was talking to Campbell about the meeting Noah had scheduled with him for breakfast tomorrow. They were supposed to be discussing a shipping agreement between their companies and Tessa was most likely paving his way.

She reached out and laid one hand on Campbell's forearm and the man smiled down at her like she was the last dessert on the table. What the hell could they be talking about for so long? And why did paving the way require touching?

"Noah?" Still frowning, he turned to say hello to Anna Morgan, the daughter of one of his biggest competitors, as she hurried up to him on four-inch heels. Morgan Bourbon was well-known stateside and Anna was no doubt here to start building connections in Europe.

"Hi," he said, shaking her hand and darting another look at Tessa and Marcus at the same time. "How are you, Anna?"

"Good, good." She tipped her head to one side. "Who are we watching?"

"What?" He reluctantly pulled his gaze from Tessa. He was more than a little annoyed to be caught staring. "No one. Just my assistant, setting up a meeting."

She looked, smiled and said, "Oh, Marcus. He's so much fun."

"Is he?" Yeah, Tessa seemed to think so, too. Frowning again, Noah forced himself to concentrate on Anna. "So, I hear your father stepped down last year and you're the CEO now."

"I am," she said, clearly pleased, as she should be. "I'm making a few changes—we'll be adding more spirits to our brand soon. I've found the most wonderful master distiller—" she broke off when it was clear his mind was elsewhere. "Never mind. We can talk business anytime. It was good to see you, Noah." She laid her right palm on his chest and leaned in to kiss his cheek. "I hope we get some time together this week."

He nodded and really looked at Anna for the first time. She was lovely, with short, dark brown hair, and big brown eyes. Her honey-colored skin was toned and muscled and she had a Southern drawl she often used to reel men in like trout. She was smart, ambitious and had a reputation for getting what she wanted. He could admire that in anyone.

But otherwise, he felt nothing. No attraction. No buzz of awareness. No heat from where her hand rested on his chest. And when she stepped back, it was a relief.

"We'll make a point of it," he said and watched her go for a long minute before turning back to Tessa and Marcus Campbell.

The two of them looked to be having a good time and that was more than annoying. Oh, Noah knew Tessa was laying groundwork with Marcus for the meeting that was coming up. But did she have to have such a good time about it? Maybe the better question was, why did it bug him so much? He was being downright territorial and that was something he'd never done. He didn't like it.

What the hell was he going to do without her? Was he crazy for starting this affair? Probably, though he couldn't really regret it.

But losing her from the company was going to be a nightmare. Hell, he hadn't even set up interviews to try to find a replacement, because how could he possibly replace a woman who knew his company as well as he did? A woman who could talk to anyone and make them comfortable? A woman who had the ability to entertain clients and find a way to connect with possible partners?

The truth was, Tessa was far more important to him—his business—than he'd ever realized. And now that he was acknowledging it, he had to let her go? He didn't think so.

She smiled at Marcus and her whole face lit up. And that smile did something to Noah that he'd never really experienced before, which told him this thing between them had to end.

An affair he could accept—welcome. A relationship was something he wasn't interested in. He had a focus already and wouldn't try to divide it between the company and a woman, only to fail at both because neither had gotten his best.

So, since he was about to lose his lover, he might as well try to keep his assistant if he could.

The Tower of London, Westminster Abbey and Buckingham Palace—it had been a full couple of hours and Tessa was loving it. The crowds in London weren't slowed down by weather so she refused to let it affect her day, either. Streets were jammed with cars and those great double-decker buses and pedestrians taking their lives in their hands darting through the traffic like ballet dancers.

It was wonderful. All of it.

"Is there anything else you want to see?" Noah asked, keeping the umbrella positioned over both of them. The rain had come back, but it hadn't stopped them from exploring. And if Tessa were honest about it, she'd admit that the rain almost made it better. Under their umbrella, they were locked together in their own little world. It felt insulated. Private.

"Actually, I'd love a cup of coffee—or tea, I guess."

Noah winced. "Tea's the safer bet. We passed a tea shop about a block back, if you're interested."

"Sure." She hooked her arm through his and they walked down the sidewalk to the rhythm of the rain beating against the umbrella. Shop windows were brightly lit and customers flowed in and out. And in a few shops, Tessa spotted the first signs of Christmas decorations.

Noah opened the door to the tea shop and ushered her in. The room was warm and dry and smelled like heaven.

They claimed a table by the front window, giving them a view of the rain-drenched street. When a waitress arrived, they ordered tea with sandwiches and scones. Tessa shrugged out of her jacket and hooked it on the back of her chair as Noah did the same.

"This was really nice of you, Noah," she said. "I never would have believed that you'd take the time to do the tourist thing."

"I can be flexible," he argued and when she only smiled, he acknowledged, "Fine. I'm as flexible as a steel pole."

"But you admit it and that's a start."

"Oh, thanks," he said with a choked off laugh.

"Anyway, knowing how you must hate this only makes me appreciate it more. I had a great time."

"Even in the rain?"

"It's atmospheric," she said.

"And freezing," he pointed out. Then he quieted while their waitress brought out a tray with a fine-china pot of tea along with two cups and saucers, a small pitcher of cream and a dish of lemon slices, as well.

She smiled at them both and said, "I'll be right back with your sandwiches and scones."

"Thank you." Tessa poured a cup of the steaming black tea. With a dollop of cream in it, it was perfect and tasted just right. She sighed at her first sip and Noah laughed.

"I get a sigh over coffee. But tea?"

"Don't knock it till you try it," Tessa teased.

Once he had, he was forced to nod. "Not bad. Especially on a day like today."

When lunch arrived, they helped themselves, and while they ate, they talked about the conference and what they'd noticed so far.

"I talked to Steph," Tessa said. "Gave her a couple of names and asked her to get Legal on them."

"That's good. I ran into Anna Morgan this morning."

"Really. How is she? Doing well as the new CEO?" Tessa knew Anna had been trying to convince her father for years to retire and hand over the reins. It seemed she'd finally gotten what she wanted.

"Seems to be," he said and poured them each more tea. "I saw you talking with Marcus Campbell."

His tone sounded weird, but Tessa ignored it. "You should have come over and said hello."

"I'll say hello at our meeting tomorrow morning." He picked up his cup. "You two seemed to have a lot to say to each other."

"Well, yeah," she said. "I haven't seen him since last year's conference. Marcus is fun to talk to."

"Is he?" One of Noah's eyebrows lifted. "His Scottish accent is so thick I can hardly understand him half the time."

Again, weird tone, but who knew what was going through his mind? Tessa chose to skip right over it and smiled. "I love his accent."

"Yeah," he muttered. "I noticed."

"Okay, what's going on with you, Noah?" she said abruptly.

"Nothing. Just wondering how close you and Marcus are."

"Close?" She laughed. "He lives in Glasgow and I live in Laguna, so not very."

"You know what I mean," Noah said.

"Yeah I do. And I'm wondering where this is coming from." She looked at him and saw he wasn't angry. If anything, he looked distant, remote, as if he was pulling back from her even while sitting still. What the heck? They'd had a nice couple of hours and he'd shown none of this. How was he able to go from fun and charming to robotic in a finger snap?

"I just told you I haven't seen Marcus since last year."

"Uh-huh. What about Travis?"

Tessa shook her head. *"Travis?"*

"He's a lot closer than Glasgow, isn't he?" Noah shrugged and leaned in closer so he could lower his voice to avoid being overheard. "You had a stock of condoms that first night we were together. And Travis seemed to know his way around you and your house."

She sat back and shook her head. What had happened? What was he thinking, and why now? In the five years she'd known Noah, she'd seen every aspect of his personality and mean wasn't a part of him. "Okay, this is going way beyond weird. Do you have a fever?"

"What? No."

"Are you sure, because you seem pretty delusional. A fever would explain it."

He scowled at her. "I don't have a fever. Just a question. How close are you and Travis?"

"That's none of your business," she said, feeling the first stirrings of her temper beginning to boil.

"That close, eh?" He nodded thoughtfully and leaned back in his chair.

"Why *yes*, Noah," she ground out and now it was her turn to lean forward. The lovely shop, the warmth of the place and the heavenly scents all seemed to wither away. Locking her gaze with his, she whispered, "You've cleverly discovered my darkest secrets. Travis is a wild lover. We meet at the full of the moon and dance naked under the elm tree in my backyard. You should see it in summer. We have fireworks."

His mouth worked as if he were biting back words he wanted to say and Tessa thought that was a very good idea. If he said anything else insulting, she might just pour what was left of their tea in his lap.

"Sarcasm? Really?" He finally asked. "That's all you've got?"

"It's all your question deserved," she snapped. "Believe it or not, I'm a grown woman who has had sex many times before I ever met you. I've had dates that went pretty well and I've brought men home— *my* home. My business. I've never questioned you about the bimbos you buy off with a serial gift of a diamond necklace—"

"They're not bimbos."

"—and I'm the one who has to wrap those stupid gifts and have them delivered. Have I ever once insulted you about your choices?"

Noah swallowed hard. "No, and I didn't mean to—"

"Well, you did." She stood up, gathered her coat and shrugged it on. "Congratulations, Noah. You took a perfectly lovely day and turned it to trash."

"Tessa, don't leave."

"I don't want to be near you right now."

"At least take the umbrella," he said and held it up.

"If I take that from you, I might put it somewhere you would find uncomfortable." Tessa headed for the door, stepped outside into the now pounding rain and welcomed it. She would need a storm of icy rain like this to quench the fire inside.

Nine

"Damn it, Tessa, wait!" Noah shouted loud enough for several people to turn and look at him, but Tessa just kept striding away. Everyone she passed gave her a wide berth, so he knew she was still furious. And why the hell wouldn't she be?

She didn't slow down a bit as he tossed money onto the table then chased after her, but his much longer legs made it easy to catch up quickly. Noah grabbed her arm and spun her around. The driving rain hammered down on him and the closed umbrella he was still clutching. "You'll get pneumonia or something—use the umbrella."

"I don't want anything from you." She pulled free and started walking again.

Noah watched her go, gritted his teeth and started to follow, when a woman came out of a shop, holding her purse over her head as a shield from the rain. He held out the umbrella and said, "Here. Take this."

She was startled, but grabbed it. He didn't stand around to watch her open it. Instead, he took off after Tessa, who was making damn good time.

Puddled water splashed up his legs as he ran after her, and with every pounding step, Noah cursed himself. He didn't know what the hell was happening to him lately. He'd never lost control like that before and didn't blame Tessa a bit for walking out. He was lucky she hadn't hit him over the head with that china pot.

"Come on, Tessa! Stop!" Then she did and that surprised him. He'd expected to have to chase her all the way back to the hotel.

Turning to face him, she demanded, "What do you want now? Have a few more insults for me?"

He took a breath and pushed his soaked hair back from his forehead. She looked miserable. Hair a thick wet rope on either side of her head, her face wet, clothes drenched and still, she was the most beautiful thing he'd ever seen. Everything in him wanted to grab her and hold her close, but he had the distinct impression that move wouldn't be appreciated.

"No. No, I don't."

"You sure?" She snapped out the question. "Was that why you were so nice all day? Is that what it was really about? Taking me to all those beautiful places? Being warm and funny and so damn charming? Were you just setting me up? Lulling me into complacency so you could start the interrogation and still feel good about yourself?"

Fury rang in her tone and flashed in her eyes and he couldn't blame her for that, either. Just like he couldn't blame himself for noting that even furious, she was breathtaking. Then what she said registered.

"Of course not!" Where the hell had that come from? He might be feeling a little crazy at the moment, but apparently he wasn't the only one.

She reached up and shoved her wet hair back from her face and gave a fierce scowl to a man who slowed down as if to enjoy the show. He hurried on. When they were relatively alone again, she asked, "Then what was that all about, Noah? Where do you get off throwing accusations like that at me?"

"I don't know." Shaking his head, Noah looked down the street, trying to gather the threads of thoughts in his mind, but they scattered at the attempt. Looking into her eyes, Noah added, "I don't know where that came from or why I said it. Damn it, Tessa, since this thing started between us, I feel like my brain's been on vacation."

People hurried past them, trying to escape a downpour that most of them had to be used to, he thought. But not he and Tessa. They stood there, facing off like a couple of crazy people in a storm.

He could still see the anger glinting in her eyes, but maybe it wasn't quite as fierce as it had been before.

"I guess I know what you mean," she muttered. "Because I've felt the same way once or twice. But I'm not going to stand still and let you dump your frustrations on me, Noah."

"I know that and you're right." Furious at himself now, Noah tried to figure out what the hell was happening to him. Tessa was still watching him. Waiting. For an explanation he couldn't find. Being jealous was way out of character for him. Being territorial about a woman was just nothing he'd ever felt before.

Hell, he wasn't happy about any of this. For the first time in his life, Noah felt out of control. He didn't like it.

"Tessa," he finally said, scrubbing one hand across his face, "I don't even know where any of that came from."

"I do," she said, tipping her head back, letting the rain splash against her face so she could meet his gaze. "It's been too good between us. For days now, we've been happy. And you couldn't stand that. So you sabotaged it."

"What does that mean?"

"It means you don't want to be happy, Noah." Taking a deep breath, Tessa let it sigh from her lungs as if her anger had drained away in a rush, leaving her exhausted. "You want to be focused on the company. Determined to build your brand. Anything that cuts into that focus has to be excised."

He wanted to argue with her, but wasn't that just what he'd been telling himself? Which told him that maybe he'd had the right idea before. End the affair and save his assistant. That was the only way to get through this. He probably didn't have much chance at keeping her at her job after all of this, but he was going to try. Because losing his lover would be hard. But losing Tessa out of his life completely was unfathomable.

Still, there was no way he was bringing that up *now*. Not exactly like their conversation had put her in a receptive mood.

But he had to say something to try to fix this. To repair what he'd broken. Over and beyond what they'd shared lately, he'd always liked her. Admired her. He didn't want that ruined.

"*Sabotage* is a little strong."

She shook her head and the rain kept falling.

Okay, trying for humor wasn't the best idea. "Look, I don't know what it is. Maybe you're right. Maybe you're not. The only thing I am sure of is that we've got to get out of the rain before we drown standing here."

"Fine." Her eyes weren't flashing now. But they weren't shining as they had been the last week or so.

Noah missed that.

* * *

The next morning, Noah and Tessa left their room together, but separate. For the first time since they'd made their bargain, there hadn't been any sex the night before and Noah had to wonder if there would be sex again anytime soon. Had they already been together for the last time? He hoped not.

It was only Tuesday. They should have had until Friday and now he wasn't sure what they had left at all.

"I'll see you later," Tessa said when the elevator hit the main lobby.

The doors swished open with a sigh and they stepped out of the silence into the dull roar of a couple thousand people, all talking at once. Used to be, these conferences energized Noah. Making new business connections, seeing old friends, picking up new and innovative ideas to push his business forward.

Now he silently wished all the people here were on the other side of the world.

"Meet for lunch?" he asked tentatively. "We can compare notes on our meetings."

"I can't," Tessa said. "I'm having lunch with Morris from the glass company."

"Right." Noah nodded. She was taking that meeting for him to get the basic information needed on his idea for a new style of bottle for their scotch line. "Okay then."

She started to leave, then stopped and looked at

him. "Noah, let's just take care of business and we can talk tonight."

By the tone of her voice, he wasn't sure he wanted to have that "talk," but what choice did they have? And maybe he should take a page from her book. Start setting the boundaries in place now. He hated it, because damn it, he'd had a good time this last week or so. Spending so much nonworking time with Tessa had introduced him to more fun than he could remember having in years.

"That's fine," he said. "Good luck with Morris."

She nodded. "Say hello to Marcus for me."

As he watched her walk away, he told himself she'd said that deliberately. To remind him of their argument. Tessa wasn't a woman to sit back and say nothing when she was pissed, and apparently there was plenty of anger still inside her from yesterday. And whose fault was that? he asked himself in disgust.

Breakfast with Marcus didn't improve his mood.

The Campbell family ran a bottling and distribution business out of Glasgow, Scotland, and Noah was interested in having more than one distributor in the UK. Though why he'd chosen Marcus was something he couldn't answer at the moment. Surely there were dozens of others who would be less aggravating.

The other man was about Noah's age and wore a clearly custom-tailored suit. His reddish brown hair was neatly trimmed, his green eyes were sharp and didn't seem to miss much. At least, Noah thought, they hadn't when they'd been locked on to Tessa yesterday.

After talking business over breakfast, they lingered over tea to hammer out a few more details. Noah was still not a fan of tea, but expertly made tea was better than badly made coffee in his opinion.

"You'll have your ever-efficient assistant Tessa contact me, then?" Marcus asked, though his Scots accent was so thick, it was hard to be sure.

Noah frowned thoughtfully. "Yes, I'll have her call you and get the information we need, then it will be up to the legal teams to come up with a contract we can both agree on."

Marcus lifted his cup and took a sip. "Oh, I don't think that'll be a problem." Setting the cup down in its matching saucer with a quiet clink of china, he mused, "I think this deal will be a benefit to both of us."

"I agree," Noah said.

"I will tell you," Marcus mused, "I've envied you your assistant."

"Really." Noah studied him and felt a now familiar curl of annoyance tighten inside him. When he'd seen Marcus and Tessa together, Noah hadn't been able to miss just how much Marcus admired her. Now he was forced to listen to the admiration?

"Oh, yes. When we ran into each other yesterday, she was a delight." Shaking his head, he smiled to himself. "She had any number of facts at the ready, off the top of her head. She's a stoater no doubt."

"She's a *what*?" Was that an insult or a compliment? Who the hell could tell? Either way, Noah didn't like it.

"A stoater, man." Marcus laughed shortly and picked up his tea again. "It's Glaswegian slang. Means she's fantastic is all. The woman's a wonder."

Noah already knew that, so he didn't need Marcus telling him so—or noticing, for that matter.

Marcus gave him a wink. "Don't say anything to her, but I'm thinking I'll talk her into having a bite with me tonight."

"Yeah, that's not going to work," Noah said with no regret at all. "We're working tonight."

"Get off, man," Marcus said. "It's a conference. There's drinking and eating and dancing to be done. You can't work all the while."

"I'll keep it in mind," Noah said tightly.

The morning bustle in the dining room ensured that there were too many people talking and laughing to allow anyone to overhear their conversation. Soft gray light slipped through windows displaying a wide view of the busy London street beyond. Big surprise, it was raining again.

Marcus gave him a long look. "Well, I'll ask her anyway. Take my chances."

"Up to you," Noah said, though it cost him. He didn't want Tessa spending time with Marcus but didn't know how he could stop it, either. Not like

Tessa was fond enough of him at the moment to pay any attention at all to what he had to say.

"You're a jammy man, Noah," Marcus was saying and that caught Noah's attention.

"I'm *jammy*?"

Marcus laughed to himself. "Glaswegian slang again, sorry. Means, you're a lucky man, having a woman like Tessa working for you as she's bloody brilliant."

Shaking his head in admiration, he sighed a little. "She makes my own Margaret seem a dafty roaster."

Noah held up one hand. "I'm not even going to ask what that one means. Are you sure Glaswegians speak English at all?"

Marcus grinned. "No we don't. We're Scots, man. And from Glasgow. We speak Weegie."

The man's constant good humor was only slightly less maddening than the sprinkling of bizarre words into a normal conversation.

Noah's frown deepened. "Weegie. Of course you do."

Tapping his fingers against the table top, Marcus asked, "So, is she happy? Tessa. At her job, I mean?"

Noah narrowed his gaze on the other man, suspicion rising. "Why?"

Marcus idly turned his teacup on its saucer. "Well, now, I might be considering making an offer, to steal her out from under you if I can."

For the first time around Marcus, Noah relaxed. "Won't work. She's already resigned—"

"Is that the truth, then?" Marcus leaned back in his chair and allowed himself a satisfied smile. "That's grand news to get on a gray morning."

"Yeah," Noah shook his head. "She quit because she has her own business she wants to devote her time to."

"A stoater, I told you," Marcus mused.

"Yeah, stoater or not, she's not going to move to Scotland to do a job she basically just quit in America."

"What's her business then?"

"She has an Etsy shop," Noah muttered, remembering the times in her kitchen, tying those stupid bows. Pouring candles and splashing hot wax on himself.

"Brilliant," Marcus crowed with a grin. "God bless the internet. She can work on her business from Glasgow as easily as she can from California."

"She'll say no," Noah said, then frowned. At least he hoped to hell she would. He understood that he couldn't have Tessa, but damned if he'd be able to stand knowing that she was living in Scotland with Marcus. But, again, it wasn't like he could prevent it.

"Won't know until I try, will I?" Marcus signaled for the check and while they waited for the waiter to appear, he said, "I'll get the check this time, as a toast to our future business together."

"Thanks…"

"And, because I'm going to try to steal your Tessa for my own, it's the least I can do." He grinned again.

Scowling, Noah muttered, "You said jammy means luck?"

"I did."

"Well, you're gonna need a lot of jam."

"I'm swimmin' in it, Noah," Marcus said, eyebrows wiggling, grin widening. "Swimmin' in it."

While Noah took his morning meeting, Tessa attended a panel on European distribution. Fascinating? Not in any way. But she was there to gather information for Noah, so she dutifully made notes on her tablet.

As the panelists took turns explaining the steps taken in distribution, Tessa paid more attention to the speakers. You could tell a lot about people by the way they spoke about their employees, their business. Pride? Disinterest? Either one was a good indicator of what it might be like dealing with them.

While three of the men spoke about themselves and how they'd single-handedly built the biggest, the best—the fourth man instead heaped praise on his truck drivers and warehouse workers, the office help and everyone else who worked for him. He spoke of himself and his employees as a team and said it had been essential in building his company.

Tessa noted his name and the name of his business. The final decision would be Noah's, or maybe Steph's, but if they didn't want her opinion, they shouldn't send her to these things.

Her phone was on vibrate and she jumped when her pocket buzzed. Glancing at the screen, she saw Stephanie's name and keeping her voice in a whisper, she said, "Hi, Steph. Everything okay?"

"It's great, are you kidding?"

The man seated in front of Tessa turned around, glared at her and huffed out, "Shh!"

Wincing, Tessa hushed out, "Hang on," then she slipped down the aisle and out the door into a lobby that was full and bustling.

Finding the nearest chair, Tessa plopped down and said, "Hi again. Okay now I can talk."

"What happened?"

"I was at a panel, couldn't talk without getting the hate stare."

"Sorry."

"Don't be," Tessa assured her. "You did me a favor. I got what I needed, anyway. I think you should check out Harry Miller of Two Brothers trucking, based in Liverpool. I really liked what he had to say and I think he'd work out well for us—well, you."

"Okay, got it, thanks. I'll have Research do a run on them and then talk to Noah."

Tessa would tell Noah when she saw him, but giving Steph a heads-up would get things moving quickly. Funny, Tessa thought, but she would miss this part of what she did, too. Being trusted to find the right people for the right job. It was a good feeling to find someone like Harry Miller, who, if he contracted with Graystone, would see a huge leap in business.

But she couldn't stay. Especially after yesterday. Things had gone so wrong so fast, Tessa still wasn't sure what had happened. He'd turned from Mr. Charm into Mr. Who-The-Heck-Is-This in a blink of time. And though he'd sort of apologized, Tessa wasn't completely mollified. How could she be?

He might not know why he'd said all those things, but she did. He was scared. Something Noah would never admit. But she could see it. As she'd told him, things had been way too good between them. They'd meshed together so well that it had been almost effortless, and for Noah, that was worrying.

Since the tea shop, things had been so tense between them, it felt as if they were just acquaintances, trapped in a luxury hotel suite without a clue how to act toward each other. Heck, Tessa hadn't even left him yet and she already missed him. Missed the closeness, the laughter… *The sex, Tessa. You also miss the sex.* Yes, she did. They'd slept in the same bed last night, but they might as well have been on different planets. There'd been no touching, cuddling, kissing.

That argument had been right there in between them, like a wall neither of them could breach. And now, they had two more full days together before they left England on Friday. That was the day that, like Cinderella running from the ball at midnight, Tessa had planned to make her escape from Noah's world.

Now she didn't know if she could make it until then if this was how it was going to be.

After taking a steadying breath, Tessa forced cheer into her voice to talk to Stephanie because she really didn't want to get into this with her friend—and Noah's sister.

"So what's going on at home?"

"You will not believe how great the walls in this place look. And the floor, once it's finished, is going to be gorgeous. They've already got half the office done."

Right. She'd forgotten about Stephanie's plan to redo the office while Noah was gone. "Wow, that was fast!"

"The word *bonus*, remember?" Stephanie laughed a little. "I even got them to come in on Sunday so we could get a jump on it all."

"I always said you were impressive."

"And you are exceptionally perceptive," Stephanie said. "Enough about the now gorgeous office. How's England? Oooh. Better yet, how's my brother?"

Tessa took the easy question first. "England is great. Of course, December weather is cold and wet…"

"Sounds lovely."

"Actually, it is." Standing, Tessa moved over to a coffee bar, waited behind two other people and managed to snag herself a cup. She smiled at the woman next to her, then went back to her surprisingly uncomfortable chair. "We went to Stonehenge on Sunday."

"I'm sorry. I don't think I heard that right. Stonehenge?" Clearly incredulous, Stephanie said, "Noah went to a tourist attraction?"

"Well, it's not an amusement park, Steph. It's historic."

"You got that right," she said. "Getting Noah to take a day off is historic."

Laughing wryly, Tessa sipped at her coffee. It had been staggering that Noah had voluntarily taken time off. And then more time yesterday… okay, don't go there.

"It was wonderful, really. Even in the rain." She took a breath and said, "Yesterday, we did the Tower, Westminster Abbey and Buckingham Palace."

"A shame it's so early here," Stephanie muttered. "I need a drink."

Smiling, Tessa said, "It was really nice."

"Uh-huh." Stephanie paused for a moment, then said, "I can hear the tone of your voice, Tessa. Something besides tourist heaven is going on. What did Noah do?"

"Why do you think it was Noah?"

"Please."

Tessa nodded and lifted one hand in a wave to a woman she knew. "Okay yes, it was Noah. Yesterday afternoon, he said some things that really made me furious and we had a big fight and now, I just don't think I'm going to make it here until Friday."

"God, he's an idiot." Stephanie's sigh was audible. "Honestly, I've found that most men are, but even in this, Noah is a standout."

"I don't know what set him off, either."

"I can guess," Stephanie said.

"So can I," Tessa agreed. "But it doesn't really matter in the grand scheme, does it? We both said some things we shouldn't have and I don't see a way back from it."

"There's always a way back if you want it badly enough."

She stared out through the windows, watching the rain falling and the people strolling along the sidewalk. A sea of umbrellas bobbed and moved with the crowd.

"I used to think that, too."

"Damn it, Tessa," Steph snapped. "You already knew Noah. You loved him anyway. So *now* you've decided you can't take it?"

That sounded too close to the truth to be comfortable. Tessa had known Noah. She knew his good side, his bad side and everything in between.

"But I quit my job, Steph," she reminded her

friend. "And this 'break' with Noah was always going to be temporary."

"It doesn't have to be."

Tessa laughed darkly. Shaking her head, she looked around the lobby and the hundreds of people milling about, chatting, studying conference schedules, sitting at the open bar. The hotel staff was busy, but everything was running smoothly. Well, she thought, not everything. She and Noah had hit a brick wall.

Everyone here at the conference had a purpose. So did she and Noah.

Once that purpose was fulfilled, what was left?

Dinner that night started out tense. Noah had spent most of the day wondering what the hell he was going to say to Tessa. And he hadn't come up with a damn thing. At the end of the week, she would be gone. Her job done. This temporary seduction over. And where was that going to leave him?

Exactly where he had been when all of this started, he assured himself. Except he wouldn't have Tessa to bounce ideas off. He wouldn't have her making sure his business and, hell, his *life* were organized. He wouldn't see her every morning or get to eat the cinnamon Christmas cake she made every year. He'd forgotten about that until just that moment and it was yet another bitter pill to swallow.

He wouldn't have Tessa. But he would still have

his family's legacy to prove. His grandfather's brand to build. Until he succeeded at that, he couldn't allow himself to consider anything else in his life.

No, he wouldn't have Tessa. She wouldn't be in his bed anymore because he'd begun to feel things for her, and that he simply couldn't allow.

"You're quiet," Tessa said, voice low, but carrying over the murmured conversations filling the hotel restaurant.

It was a palatial room. Tiled floors, cream-colored walls with images of England dotting those walls. Tuxedoed waiters moved between the small round tables and more private booths. There was subtle music filling the air from a pianist in the center of the room. Lighting was muted, with candles flickering on every table and hidden lighting along the crown molding on the ceiling. It was a stunning place and the food was delicious, yet it might as well have been cardboard for all Noah had tasted it.

Losing Tessa from his bed *and* his office was too much, so Noah was going to take a chance. "I've been doing some thinking."

He turned in the booth to face her and his breath stopped. Tessa was beautiful every day. But in candlelight, she was stunning. Shadows danced on her skin and flames flickered in her eyes. Her hair was loose, across her shoulders bared by the narrow straps of a black dress that boasted a short skirt and a diving neckline that kept capturing his attention.

"So have I," she said. "I wonder if we're thinking the same thing."

"Let's find out." He took a sip of wine, set the glass down again and met Tessa's gaze. "I want you to stay on at your job."

Tessa laughed shortly, then took a sip of her own wine and shook her head. "Well, question answered. We're not thinking of the same thing."

He frowned and had to wonder what had been in her mind. But he only said, "That's not an answer."

"You already know the answer, Noah," she said, shaking her hair back from her face. "I can't stay."

"Yes, you can," he said and told her what he'd come up with during the long day they'd spent apart. Noah knew he'd have to be damn good at this since he'd insulted her earlier.

"We'll write up a contract. Have Legal draw it."

"For what?"

"To lay out your hours," he said, warming to his theme. "What's expected of you at the job. No more on call twenty-four/seven, Tessa."

"Noah…"

"Just hear me out." He rubbed one hand across the back of his neck and forced himself to say, "I'm sorry. About before. I don't even have an explanation for what I said so maybe you were right to a point. That I was sabotaging us, I mean."

"Thanks for the apology. Really. I know the word *sorry* doesn't really hop into your lexicon very often."

"Because I'm rarely wrong," he said and smiled, hoping to ease some of the tension simmering between them. "Tessa, this affair or whatever it is we're doing is coming to an end."

She stiffened. He saw it and didn't like it. "We both knew that going in," he added.

"We did."

"But you can keep your job," he insisted. "We're adults. We can handle working together and not sleeping together. You'll have shorter hours, weekends off. You can get that dog you want and you can still be a part of Graystone." He was talking faster now, because he could feel that he was losing her. "Damn it, Tessa, you're good at it. You know the company almost as well as I do.

"And look what you've accomplished here at the conference alone. You've lined up two distributors and already have Legal looking into them. You set up that meeting with Marcus for me. You're good at this. Beyond good. I need you at work, Tessa. Stay."

She was watching him and he wished to hell he could read what was in her mind. But at least he didn't have to wait long to find out.

"No."

He jerked his head back. Hell, he'd made a lot of accommodation in his offer. Short hours, weekends off. What more could he do? "Just no? That's it?"

"Yes." She took a sip of her wine and lifted her chin. "That's it. I'm not staying, Noah. I can't."

"Why the hell not?"

She looked at him and the candle flame flickering there danced and swayed. "Because I love you."

Noah jerked back in his seat. This he hadn't expected. At all. He'd prepared himself to counter whatever argument she would give him, but this one had never crossed his mind. "Love?"

"Wow," she said with a broken laugh. "Way to nail the deer-in-the-headlights-expression." Sighing a little, she added, "Relax, Noah. You don't owe me anything. You don't even have to say anything."

"I don't know what to say," he admitted. Hell, no one but his mother had ever said those words to him. But to be fair, he'd lived his life in a way to avoid any kind of entanglement that might end with that particular admission.

"You know what?" She took another sip of wine and set her glass down again. "We started all this because I wanted to kiss you at least once. Remember?"

"Yeah, I do." That first kiss was still seared into his memory.

"Well," she said, "I wanted to say *I love you* once, too. I don't need anything from you, Noah. I just wanted to tell you *why* I won't keep working for you. I love you and you'll never love me—" she shrugged "—so I can't stay. I can't keep working for you, knowing what we had for a week and will never have again."

"Tessa—" He had to say *something*. But everything that raced through his mind just wasn't right.

Noah didn't want to hurt her, but he couldn't make her the kind of promises she wanted from him.

"Oh, stop it, Noah," she said on a huff.

Surprised again, he asked, "Stop what?"

"Scrambling for something to say that won't hurt poor little Tessa."

"I wasn't—" He broke off, unable to deny it. "Fine. I was."

"I know." Her mouth curved. "You're not the mystery you think you are, Noah."

He didn't know how to take that, either. All he knew for sure was that this dinner hadn't gone the way he'd wanted it to—and Tessa loved him.

"Look," she said and Noah stopped thinking and started listening. "You and I had a wonderful time this last week, and that's how I want to end this. We can part friends and just move on."

"So I just let you walk away."

"You can't stop me," she said and her smile dissolved as she shook her head. "And if you're honest with yourself, if not with me…that's exactly what you want to do."

Before Noah could answer, a man's voice cut into the conversation.

"Excuse me. I don't mean to interrupt."

Noah gritted his teeth and swiveled his head to look at Marcus Campbell. He hadn't heard the man approach and now he wondered how long he'd been standing there. "What is it, Marcus?"

The man grinned and looked from Noah to

Tessa. "I just wanted to ask Tessa if she would join me for a drink. Say in about an hour? I've something I'd like to talk to you about."

"Uh," she said, glancing at Noah before saying, "sure, I guess. The hotel bar?"

"Grand," Marcus said. "See you then." He nodded. "Noah."

"Marcus," he ground out and watched the man walk away before turning to Tessa and blurting out, "He wants to offer you a job."

"Really?" Clearly amused, she smiled.

"I told him you wouldn't be interested," he admitted.

"Did you?" She tipped her head to one side and stared at him.

Astounded, he asked, "Was I wrong? You'll quit working for me, but you'll move to Glasgow and work for Campbell?" There was absolutely no way he'd be able to deal with that.

"I won't know that until I hear his offer, will I?"

"Seriously?" It was a challenge to keep his voice low enough that it wouldn't carry beyond their booth, because frustration had Noah by the throat and was currently squeezing. "I can't give you what you want and you leave the *country*?"

Tessa's eyebrows lifted high on her forehead. "Wow. Believe it or not, Noah, this isn't about *you*."

"Of course it is. We have an argument, I make an ass of myself and you go to work in *Glasgow*."

Abruptly, she held up both hands and said,

"You know what? Let's not. One argument a day is really my limit."

"Tessa." He reached out, grabbed one of her hands and held on. "I am sorry. About earlier. About now. I wish it could be different."

She lifted one hand and cupped his cheek. "No you don't, Noah. Or you would *make* it different."

He looked into her eyes and knew it was over. Whatever they'd shared this last week and more was done. Maybe it was the stupid argument and everything he'd said when his insides were churning with too many unfamiliar emotions and thoughts. And maybe it was just time for it to end.

He felt a cold hand squeezing his heart and didn't want to think about why it was happening. Noah felt the warmth of her hand on his face and let the heat of her touch slide into him for what would probably be the last time.

What felt like a great black hole opened up inside him and Noah knew it would be with him for a long time.

Ten

"You could work for me in Glasgow," Marcus said later, giving Tessa a warm, tempting smile.

But she was immune to charm and temptation now. Tessa knew who she loved and she knew he didn't love her back. What did she care about a different man's charm?

She'd thrown herself and her heart into the affair with Noah on the theory that if she'd been with him, she could at last walk away with some sort of satisfaction. Instead, she was left feeling emptier and colder and more alone than ever. She'd lost. Her job. Her heart. Her time with Noah. And now, she just wanted to be home, working on her business, doing normal things until that normal finally spilled into her soul and began to heal her.

"I appreciate the offer, Marcus. Really." She shook her head slowly and added, "But I'm not looking for another job."

There were a lot of people in the bar for a late-night drink and the music streaming through the speakers added a layer of cheer that Tessa just wasn't feeling.

"If not a job, why not an adventure?" Marcus leaned toward her and his eyes were fixed on hers. "Move to Glasgow for a year. Work for me—you'll have time for the business Noah says is so important to you—"

"He did?" Well, at least he'd listened to something she'd said.

"We've the internet in Scotland, too, you know. You could be happy there, Tessa. And I'd best whatever salary you were making at Noah's company."

"It's not about the money, Marcus. Really." She stirred her martini with the swizzle stick and watched the liquid slide around the inside of the glass as if hypnotized.

"Ah," he said. "So it's like that, is it?"

"What?" She looked at him.

"You're in love with the man."

"Am I that obvious?"

"Maybe not to everyone." He slapped one hand to his heart and sighed heavily. "This is a great disappointment to me. It's shattered my plans completely."

Tessa had to smile. Marcus Campbell was a man who knew how attractive he was and played it up for whatever woman was handy. And right now, his undeniable charisma was directed solely at her, so she had to admit it was a formidable weapon. At any other point in her life, she would have been enjoying herself. Marcus was gorgeous, fun, and oh my, that accent. But as long as she was in love with Noah, no other man interested her.

"Sorry your plans took a hit," she said, smiling. "I do appreciate the offer, though."

He waved that off. "I'll recover." Then he stared into her eyes. "Will you?"

Tessa took a sip of her martini and it tasted like dust. "Eventually."

Sighing again, Marcus drained the last of his drink, set the glass down and said, "Earlier today I told Noah that he was a lucky man. Now I'm thinking a man so foolish as to let you go, doesn't deserve luck."

"Why didn't I fall in love with you, Marcus?" A sad smile curved her mouth.

He reached out and gave her hand a quick pat. "A mystery to me, as well."

Tessa laughed as he'd meant her to and she was grateful.

Wednesday night was the big award ceremony, but Tessa wasn't attending in the mood she'd thought she would be. She was there, with Noah, but they were so separate, it was heartbreaking. At least, it was to her.

Noah seemed unaffected, which was exactly what she'd expected from him. He was so determined to avoid any kind of entanglement, she was only surprised he hadn't put her on the private jet to fly her home the moment she'd confessed that she loved him. As it was, she'd moved her things into the second bedroom of their suite and even the much smaller bed felt the size of a football field without him lying next to her. She hadn't slept much, so she was on edge and trying not to show it.

Tessa had worked alongside Noah for a long time, and this award ceremony had always been the carrot at the end of the stick. If the varietal vodka won tonight, Noah would have reached his first goal for honoring his grandfather.

She wondered if that award would be enough for him. Would he relax a bit, enjoy the win and start to wake up to life around him? Or, more likely, it would only focus him further in the race to capture *every* vodka award. To make the name Graystone interchangeable with the word *vodka*.

She glanced at him, sitting beside her in the crowded ballroom. There was dessert and champagne being served by silent, efficient waiters. A formal affair, the men in the crowd wore tuxedos and the women were dressed spectacularly in long, gorgeous gowns, with their necks and arms draped in priceless jewels.

Tessa's own dress, a deep scarlet, was strapless, clinging to her upper body and then sliding down the rest of her body in a bell shape. Her necklace had been made by Lynn, with faux rubies and diamonds, and the matching earrings completed the set.

Noah hadn't been able to hide the admiration in his gaze when she'd joined him in the suite, but since arriving at the awards, he'd hardly looked at her. Pain poked at her, but she ignored it. *Get used to it, Tessa. The fun and games are over and now it's back to grim reality.*

Except, her reality wasn't grim at all. And now she'd have the time to enjoy her life. Grow her business. Visit with her friends. And, in every other waking moment, miss Noah so much she would ache with it.

She took a breath, blew it out and reached for her flute of champagne. After a quick swallow, she felt she could speak and used her chance to say quietly, "Good luck, Noah."

He looked at her, so sternly handsome, her heart twisted. For one brief moment, his eyes warmed and she wished that moment would last forever. But then it was gone and he said only, "Thank you, Tessa. And whatever happens tonight, thank you for all your hard work in the past."

She nodded, because what could she say to that? Tessa felt as if he'd just handed her a gold watch and waved her off into retirement. There was no connection between them at all anymore. He'd sealed it off and she had to wonder again how he was capable of doing it so cleanly.

She'd seen him shut out other women over the years, but she'd never realized just how painful it could be.

For the next hour, they applauded politely for the winners and drank from the constantly refilled champagne glasses. But finally, the varietal vodka awards were announced. Tessa sensed Noah's tension and she shared it. No matter what had happened between them, she hoped Graystone Vodka won because Noah had worked so hard and for so long to reach this goal. As the master of ceremonies read off the finalists, Tessa reached out and laid her hand over Noah's. He instantly turned his hand over and closed his fingers over hers.

"The varietal vodka award goes to…Graystone Vodka for their Blackberry and Lime infusion."

Noah squeezed her hand hard, then released her and stood up to move through the room, accepting congratulations along the way. When he reached the stage, Tessa applauded with the crowd and watched as he accepted the gold medallion that he'd devoted most of his life to claiming. When he left the stage, people rushed to congratulate him and Tessa watched from afar as he accepted accolades from his peers.

I'm happy for him. Really happy. Then Anna Morgan rushed up to Noah and threw her arms around his neck. Tessa waited for Noah to break away, but instead, he threw himself into the moment, wrapped his arms around Anna and swung her in a circle while she laughed and his friends erupted into more cheers.

Tessa couldn't watch anymore. She grabbed her purse and headed out of the crowded room. The noise was deafening and she felt as if she were drowning in it all. Despite the heat of the room, she felt cold right down to her bones. For one brief moment when Noah had squeezed her hand, she'd felt that they were still a team. That they were in this together. But then he was gone and so was the moment.

Tessa didn't belong there anymore.

When Noah finally made it back to their table, Tessa was gone. He looked for her, but came up empty. After an hour spent accepting congratulations and looking for Tessa in the crowd, he at last took the elevator to their suite. But she wasn't there, either. Her room was empty. Suitcase gone. She'd left. Without a word.

"Why the hell would she leave?" he muttered, looking around fruitlessly for some kind of note. But there was nothing. It was as if she'd never been there at all.

"Fine then," he said aloud to the room, "no goodbye it is."

Noah stood in the shadows, his tuxedo jacket

tossed across the nearest chair. He held on to the medallion he'd worked so hard to win and felt the heavy, cold metal bite into his skin. He looked down at it and the glint of gold winked up at him. This was the culmination of years. The settling of a debt he owed to the grandfather he loved.

He should be happy, damn it.

"Congratulations, Noah," he muttered. "You won."

"For the love of God," Stephanie said, two weeks later, letting her head drop to her desk top. "Go see Tessa. Talk to her. Please stop talking to *me*."

Noah stopped pacing in his sister's office and glared at her, even though she couldn't see it. "Tessa has nothing to do with this," he grumbled. "It's my new assistant. She keeps crying when she talks to me."

"I know the feeling," Stephanie muttered and lifted her head. "She's new, Noah. It's going to take her some time to get the hang of the job."

"She shouldn't even be here. It should be Tessa at that desk."

Tessa should be in his bed. In his arms.

"Well, Tessa's not. She quit and you let her go."

"This is *my* fault?" he countered.

"Of course it is." Stephanie took a breath and sighed it out. "She loves you, you love her and you were too cowardly to do anything about it."

That stopped him dead as he fired his sister

a look that should have terrified her. But didn't. "Cowardly?"

"What would you call it?" Stephanie stood up. "You have that award you've been talking about for years. You have a woman who loves you enough to put up with you, which is damn near heroic if you ask me..." He opened his mouth, but she held up one hand to keep him quiet because clearly she wasn't finished. "And you let her go, rather than admit that some things are more important than a promise you made when you were fourteen years old."

That slapped at him. Noah had vowed to his grandfather that he would restore the Graystone name. And he'd finally gotten to the point where he could make good on that promise. So he was supposed to stop? "So I just forget about Papa and what I owe him? What we owe him?"

"Nobody's saying that. You can have both, you know," Stephanie said. "You can succeed in business *and* love someone."

He shook his head. He'd done nothing but think about this since he returned from England and his mind kept going in circles. He hated being in his own damn home now because it was gigantic and empty and the silence seemed to mock him every time he entered. All he could think about was that cottage in Laguna where Tessa was, with light and warmth and...Tessa. Angrily, he shoved both hands through his hair and said, "You don't get it, Steph."

"Of course I get it, you idiot," she said and affection colored her tone in spite of her words. "We were raised by the same people. In the same house. Who else *could* get it?"

"Fine. Then you understand. I can't have Tessa and keep the vow I made to Papa."

"Okay," she said patiently, "let's try a new tactic. Who built this business?"

"Papa, of course."

"And was he a bachelor?"

"Are you delirious? No." He didn't know where she was going with this, but if she was trying to calm him down, she was doing a poor job of it.

"Exactly." Stephanie came around her desk, then sat on the edge of it to talk to him. "He was married to Nana for fifty-eight years until she died."

"What's your point?"

"Seriously? My point is, he had a full life *and* he built this company," she snapped. "He managed to love his wife and his idiot son and all of his grandchildren and *still* build a successful company. You think Papa would love knowing that you're sacrificing everything to keep a vow you made as a hurting kid?"

Was she right? Was he being an ass about all of this, refusing to take a risk on love and using the vow to his grandfather as an excuse?

Tension was still coiled inside him like a snake, ready to strike at his heart. His soul. Yet, as he stared at his sister, Noah felt as though something else was opening up inside him. Not enough to push aside the anger, the frustration and the damn ache that losing Tessa had caused him.

But enough to toss a little light into the shadows within.

"You talked to Stephanie again, didn't you?"

Tessa stopped wrapping the jasmine soaps and looked up at Lynn. "How can you tell?"

"Because you're a tiny bit happy. You've got this little satisfied smile on your face," Lynn said. "Being a gifted detective, this tells me Noah's sister has been telling you that the man is still miserable."

Really, Tessa thought, she had to work on her poker face. She was far too easy to read. And Lynn was right. Tessa had talked to Stephanie a few times since she'd been back from England. Which was how she knew that Noah was crabby and arguing with everyone.

She shouldn't be happy about that, but she was. Did that make her petty? If so, she could live with that.

"But that's the thing," she said as if she'd said all of that aloud, "he should be happy. He won the award. That's been his goal for years."

"Maybe he figured out that it's not as important as he once thought it was," Lynn said.

Tessa thought about that for a moment, then shook her head. "No. That was always Noah's driving force."

"Well, maybe losing you and winning the award

on the same night took some of the shine off it. Besides, things change." Lynn waved a hand at the table, the island they were standing next to and the kitchen counter. Labeled boxes were stacked everywhere but the island where the two of them were still packing. "Look at you. Two weeks of having the time to work on the business and it's already taking off."

"Well, the internet ads haven't hurt, either," Tessa said. "But okay, you're right. I can see that. And it's been great. Being home. Working with you." She took a deep breath and let it out again. "Look at us. A week before Christmas and we're sending out maybe three times the product we did last year."

Then she went quiet and let her mind fill, as it had so often lately, with images of Noah, and their time together. It should make her smile, but it didn't because it was all over. And that was crazy, too, because she should be happy. She was working for herself. Now that she had the time, her business was growing. And she wasn't on call for Noah every minute of the day, and that, she thought, was why she wasn't happy.

She missed him. Tessa sighed. She would always miss him.

"You're doing it again."

Tessa looked over at Lynn. "What am I doing?"

"Sighing." Shaking her head, her friend said,

"You have that sad smile on your face and your eyes went all soft."

"Well, don't I sound gorgeous?" Tessa muttered and cut off another ten inches of ribbon, this time yellow, to go with the jasmine soaps.

"Always," Lynn said with a smile. "So where were you?"

"At Stonehenge." Tessa shrugged. "It was great that day. Pounding rain, icy wind—"

"Yeah, sounds wonderful," Lynn said with a short laugh.

"I guess you had to be there." That day was only one of the memories that played over and over in her mind. Tessa tied the bow and moved on to the next order. Stacking three bars of yellow-and-white hand-cut soaps, she slipped the ribbon beneath them and tied the stack together.

This was what Tessa had wanted. But it wasn't turning out as she had hoped. Oh, she was making more sales and that was good, but there wasn't the joy she used to feel when she was working at home. Probably because she couldn't stop thinking about Noah.

"Have you heard anything from him?" Lynn's voice was soft, almost tentative.

"It's okay," Tessa said, "you can say his name. And no, haven't heard a word from Noah. But then, I didn't expect to."

"Really?" Lynn set the wrapped jewelry box aside and leaned against the kitchen island. "But from everything you told us, it seems to me that he was having as good a time as you were."

"He did." Tessa smiled at her friend. "Which is exactly why he's not talking to me now."

"That makes zero sense."

"Welcome to the world of Noah." Tessa smiled ruefully. He wouldn't spend any time exploring memories as she was. For Noah, when something was over, he was finished with it. Sad as it was to admit, he probably hadn't given her a second thought since they'd been home.

Suddenly tired of her own thoughts, Tessa set the last of the wrapped soaps aside, and asked, "Coffee?"

"Sure."

Tessa always had a fresh pot of coffee going, so she poured two cups, handed one to Lynn, then said, "Let's sit for a minute. I have some cookies my wonderful neighbor made me."

Lynn laughed. "Ah, my chocolate chips. They're all gone at my house. Carol says it's all Evan, but she gets up in the middle of the night to snack and thinks I don't know."

Tessa laughed and set the cookies in the center of the table. "Well, then, I'm glad I saved some for you."

"Me, too." Lynn took a bite then waved her cookie. "So tell me about the weird world of Noah."

"Not really weird," she allowed. "It all makes perfect sense to him."

"Okay…"

Tessa told Lynn about Noah and his father and grandfather and how he'd been working for years to make his late grandfather proud. "That's been the one thing driving him for most of his life. And now that he's won the varietal vodka award, there'll be no stopping him. He'll want to win for each of the other vodkas, as well."

"Sounds like obsession rather than devotion to duty," Lynn mused.

"It's not, really. He's just über-focused," Tessa said, wondering why she was still defending the man. She remembered sitting next to him on award night, feeling the tension radiating from him. That prize had meant everything to him and when he'd won, he'd been so proud.

And then he'd hugged Anna Morgan and— She broke that memory off fast. "Anyway, for him, he can't bring himself to make promises to a woman if he feels he can't keep them because of what he owes to the company. And his grandfather."

"Wow. You're being really reasonable here, Tessa. Almost unbearably so."

"I'm trying." Wryly, she smiled and added, "It's taken me a long time to get to this place and I'm really trying to stay there. Lynn, it doesn't do me any good at all to stay angry at Noah.

"What would be the point? He's already gone from my life, so staying furious only hurts me, not him."

"Again. So mature." Lynn studied her. "If it were me, I'd be throwing things and putting a curse on Carol. Your stability is starting to feel a little creepy."

"Would it make you feel better if I told you I have a Noah doll that I stick pins in occasionally?"

"Sadly yes," she admitted. "It would."

"Fine," Tessa said on a laugh. "I'll get one."

"Sure. So, a new subject."

"Thank you," Tessa said. It was bad enough that her thoughts and dreams were filled with Noah. She didn't want to keep talking about him, too. It just hurt too much.

"Have you decided to adopt Hugo?"

"I did…" She sipped at her coffee, then reached for a cookie. "He was perfect. A black Lab mix, two years old and I loved that little face. You remember, I showed you Hugo's picture."

"He is cute."

"Anyway, I finally decided to adopt him and I called them this morning. But someone else had adopted him already."

"Really?" Lynn shook her head and took a drink of coffee. "I'm sorry about that. But the right dog will find you."

She laughed a little. "We'll see. I am going to spread out, though. Try a shelter in Long Beach next week."

"Uh-huh." Lynn took a bite of the cookie. "So

you're just fine and happy and moving on with your life."

"Absolutely." Tessa lifted her chin, plastered a brave, bright smile on her face and nodded.

"And," Lynn said, "you're lying."

Her shoulders slumped, her smile faded and she muttered, "Absolutely."

She couldn't move on until she got over Noah, and that, Tessa told herself sadly, was just never going to happen.

Two days later, Tessa was alone in the house when pounding erupted at her front door. After she jolted and clutched at her chest, she peeked out the front window and saw Noah's car parked outside the house.

Heartbeat suddenly pounding louder than his demanding knock, Tessa hurried to the door and threw it open. She stared up into his dark blue eyes blazing with heat and asked, "What are you doing here, Noah?"

"I'm done, Tessa. That's it. I've had it."

"What're you talking about?" He looked as handsome as ever in a pair of black jeans, boots and a dark green long-sleeved shirt. His hair was tousled as if he'd been stabbing his fingers through it and his jaw was tight, muscles flexing as if he were gritting his teeth.

It threw her off for a moment because she was so used to seeing him calm, cool, in control and wearing one of the suits that looked so amazing on him.

"I'm talking about *you*," he said, then paced to the edge of the porch and back again. "It's been two weeks and I'm still pissed. We won that damn award in England and you didn't even stick around to celebrate."

"That's what this visit is about?" She frowned at the memory of him swinging Anna Morgan around in circles in front of everyone. "It looked as though you and Anna were doing a good job of it without me."

He gaped at her, clearly stunned. "*That's* why you left? Hell, I only held on to the woman for a damn minute because at first I thought she was *you*, rushing up to share in the prize."

"Me? Come on." She didn't believe that for a second.

"If you'd stuck around," he told her, "you'd have seen me drop her like a rock and go looking for you."

Tessa was staggered by that and for the first time ever, didn't know what to say. Had she read the situation all wrong? Had she been so wrapped up in her own pain that she'd missed seeing the truth? But she stopped thinking and started listening because Noah wasn't finished yet.

"Then I got up to our suite and you were gone. Just…poof." He scrubbed one hand against the back of his neck. "Not even a damn note, Tessa. I had to find out from the concierge that you'd left for the airport."

"I almost left one," she said, but she'd convinced herself there was nothing left to say. Now she felt terrible.

"Almost doesn't count. But that's not why I'm here anyway, damn it." He frowned at her and blew out another sigh of frustration.

"Why don't we go inside and you can tell me. We don't have to stand on the porch."

"I'm not going anywhere until I say what I came to say," he ground out. And he didn't look happy about it.

"Fine," she said, crossing her arms over her chest in a clearly defensive posture. "Say it."

"The thing is, I'm here because I have a crappy new assistant who can't do the job without crying."

"Why do I care about that?" Okay, she did care, but she didn't want him to know it.

"Because it's your fault." He threw both hands up in the air helplessly. "She cries if I look at her. Cries if she can't get the printer to work. I swear, the whole office is going to be under water if this keeps up."

Tessa swallowed her smile, but not fast enough.

"Sure," he said, nodding. "You can laugh. You're not dealing with the mess you left behind when you resigned."

"You can't be blaming me," she argued.

"No, I'm blaming *me*." He took a breath and said, "Nothing's been right since you left, Tessa."

She liked hearing that. It made her heart a little

less achy to know he missed her, but still. "I don't want my old job back, Noah."

"I'm not offering you your old job," he said, and grabbed her elbows.

From somewhere down the street, Christmas carols played softly and the cold wind off the ocean slid down the narrow road, rattling naked tree limbs.

"What's this about?" she asked, looking up into his eyes.

"I want you to come back to work," he said. "And I want you to marry me."

"What?" She pulled out of his grasp and shook her head. She couldn't believe this. Thinking back to all of the bribes he'd tried to use to get her to stay with the company, she felt her temper soar. "Noah, this is ridiculous and maybe the worst thing you've ever done. You offered to remodel my house and buy me a car and give me a raise to stay and keep working for you. But offering *marriage* as a job perk is really going too far."

"What? No." He scrubbed both hands over his face. "This is coming out all wrong. That's your fault, too."

"How?"

"Because you seriously messed me up when you left. I can't even think anymore!" Scowling furiously, he continued, "Marrying me isn't a perk, Tessa. Hell, it's practically a *sentence*. I'm not an easy person."

"True."

His frown deepened at her instant agreement.

"And marriage to me will probably be hard," he added, "but I don't care, and you shouldn't either since you already admitted that you love me."

"I did, but—"

"Yeah, well, what you don't know is that I love you, too."

Tessa's knees buckled a little. She couldn't believe she was standing on her front porch, hearing the man she loved tell her he felt the same way.

"That's right. I love you. I need you," he added, "and damn it, I will have you."

Tessa had to laugh. He looked so frustrated and so...good. "You're such a romantic. I had no idea."

"You want romance? I can do romance. I brought you flowers, but I left them in the damn car and now they're probably gone."

"What?"

"Never mind. Marry me, Tessa." He reached out for her again, dropping his hands on her shoulders until the heat of his touch seeped down and into her bones, chasing away the chill she'd been living with since she left England.

"Look, I like that you've got your own business," he said. "I'll help whenever I can, but I won't tie bows anymore because mine always look like crap—"

"Agreed," she said, laughing.

"I can do romance, Tessa." His voice dropped until it was a low rumble against her heart. "I love you. I want you back working with me. Living with me. Loving me."

Tessa hardly knew what to say. He was offering her everything and all she could do was stare into those eyes of his. He wasn't hiding anything from her now. She read what he was feeling on his face. He loved her. He really did. "What about your vow to your grandfather?"

His features tightened. "I'll still make that come true. But it finally dawned on me that it was you and I together who won that award. We're a team, Tessa. One too good to break up. Together, we'll make Graystone the only vodka worth drinking."

Her heart was melting. She could feel it going soft and gooey in her chest and it was the best feeling ever. "Oh, Noah…"

"Just say yes. Damn it, Tessa, I love you! And you love me!"

Tessa smiled and said, "I'll still want to keep my own business…"

"Of course," he said, eager to please. "I'll help any way I can, like I said."

"I'll come back to the office, but only part-time."

"That works for me," he said. "I'll transfer Crying Girl to Stephanie's office."

"That's just mean."

"Tessa," he said, leaning down to rest his forehead against hers. "Marry me."

"You'll have to go to Wyoming with me to meet my family."

"Wouldn't miss it," he said and his mouth began to curve into that satisfied smile she loved so much.

"And I'll want kids."

"As many as you want," he agreed, lifting his head to nod as he looked at the house and yard before turning back to meet her gaze. "But not in my house. I think we should live here. In your castle."

"Really?" Her heart finished melting and sent rivers of warmth coursing through her bloodstream. She could marry Noah and stay in her castle and have children and love and everything she'd ever dreamed of. This was really the best day of her life. "You want to live here?"

"Yeah, I really like it, though we might have to add on at some point. And, he'll need a fenced yard—"

"What? He who?"

"In a minute." Noah dug into his pocket and came up with a pale blue box. He opened it up and showed her a sapphire-and-diamond ring. "Will you marry me, Tessa?"

Tessa's breath caught in her chest and she lifted one hand to her trembling mouth. It was happening. Her dreams were falling at her feet and all she had to do was pick them up and hold them close. She had to trust that Noah loved her and meant the promise he was making and it was so easy to do.

"Yes, Noah. I will marry you."

He grinned and slid the ring onto her finger,

then sealed it with a kiss. "I do love you," he said. "Maybe I always have."

"Just so long as you always will," she said, reaching up to cup his cheek.

"Always," he whispered and leaned in for a kiss.

That kiss ended a few seconds later, when loud, insistent barking erupted out of nowhere. Tessa looked toward his car. "What's going on?"

"Hold on—I'll be right back. He's probably eating the back seat."

Tessa watched him run to the car, open the back door and reach inside. When he stood up again, he was holding a bedraggled bouquet of flowers in one arm and a squirming black dog in the other.

"Oh, my..." Rushing off the porch, she reached Noah in seconds, then scooped the dog out of his arms. About twenty pounds of love wriggling against her. "I don't believe this. It's Hugo. The dog I wanted to adopt from the shelter."

The Lab licked her cheeks, her eyes and anywhere he could reach as he wiggled with joy. Tessa laughed in delight and looked up at Noah. "How do you have him? You're the one who adopted him?"

"Yeah." He looked at what had once been an expensive bouquet, then scowled at the dog. "I've been talking to Lynn a bit—"

"You have?" Oh, her neighbor was sneakier than Tessa would have believed.

"Yes. And she told me you wanted Hugo, so I went and got him as a surprise—and kind of a bonus for if you said yes. We'll have to watch him every second, though." He frowned at the dog. "He ate my couch at my place. Hell, he eats *everything*." He stared at the bouquet that was now mostly stems. "Including roses, apparently."

She laughed and snuggled the dog. "We'll train him. Noah, I can't believe you did all of this."

Tessa wrapped one arm around Noah's waist and held on to Hugo with the other. She tipped her head back to stare up at him and basked in the warmth of his smile. "I've loved you for so long. I can't believe this is really happening."

"Believe it."

"All because I wanted to kiss you at least once."

He grinned and kissed her again. "We wasted five years, Tessa. You should have seduced me sooner."

* * * * *

If you loved this story, try these other
fun and flirty romances from
USA TODAY *bestselling author Maureen Child!*

Temptation at Christmas
Jet Set Confessions
Red Hot Rancher
Bombshell for the Boss
Tempt Me in Vegas

WE HOPE YOU ENJOYED
THIS BOOK FROM

H HARLEQUIN
DESIRE

*Luxury, scandal, desire—welcome to
the lives of the American elite.*

Be transported to the worlds of oil barons, family dynasties,
moguls and celebrities. Get ready for juicy plot twists,
delicious sensuality and intriguing scandal.

6 NEW BOOKS AVAILABLE EVERY MONTH!

#2803 THE TROUBLE WITH BAD BOYS
Texas Cattleman's Club: Heir Apparent
by Katherine Garbera
Landing bad boy influencer Zach Benning to promote Royal's biggest soiree is a highlight for hardworking Lila Jones. And the event's marketing isn't all that's made over! Lila's sexy new look sets their relationship on fire... Will it burn hot enough to last?

#2804 SECOND CHANCE COUNTRY
Dynasties: Beaumont Bay • by Jessica Lemmon
Country music star Cash Sutherland hasn't seen Presley Cole since he broke her heart. Now a journalist, she's back in his life and determined to get answers he doesn't want to give. Will their renewed passion distract her from the truth?

#2805 SEDUCTION, SOUTHERN STYLE
Sweet Tea and Scandal • by Cat Schield
When Sienna Burns gets close to CEO Ethan Watts to help her adopted sister, she's disarmed by his Southern charm, sex appeal...and insistence on questioning her intentions. Now their explosive chemistry has created divided loyalties that may derail all her plans...

#2806 THE LAST LITTLE SECRET
Sin City Secrets • by Zuri Day
It's strictly business when real estate developer Nick Breedlove hires interior designer—and former lover—Samantha Price for his new project. Sparks fly again, but Samantha is hiding a secret. And when he learns the truth about her son, she may lose him forever...

#2807 THE REBEL HEIR
by Niobia Bryant
Handsome restaurant heir Coleman Cress has always been rebellious—in business and in relationships. Sharing a secret no-strings affair with confident Cress family chef Jillian Rossi is no different. But when lust becomes something more, can their relationship survive meddling exes and family drama?

#2808 HOLLYWOOD EX FACTOR
LA Women • by Sheri WhiteFeather
Security specialist Zeke Mitchell was never interested in the spotlight. When his wife, Margot Jensen, returns to acting, their marriage ends...but the attraction doesn't. As things heat up, are the problems of their past too big to overlook?

"Did you expect me to sleep in here with you?"

And there it was. The line that he hadn't thought to draw but now was obvious he'd need to draw.

He eased back on the bed, shoved a pillow behind his back and curled her into his side. Arranging the blankets over both of them, he leaned over and kissed her wild hair, smiling against it when he thought about the tangles she'd have to comb out later. He hoped she thought of why they were there when she did.

"We should talk about that, yeah?" he asked rhetorically. He felt her stiffen in his arms. "I want you here, Pres. In this bed. Naked in my arms. I want you on my dock, driving me wild in that tiny pink bikini. But we should be clear about what this is...and what it's not."

She shifted and looked up at him, her blue eyes wide and innocent, her lips pursed gently. "What it's not."

"Yeah, honey," he continued, gentler than before. "What it's not."

"You mean…" She licked those pink lips and rested a hand tenderly on his chest. "You mean you aren't going to marry me and make an honest woman out of me after that?"

Cash's face broadcasted myriad emotions. From what Presley could see, they ranged from regret to nervousness to confusion and finally to what she could only describe as "oh, shit." That was when she decided to let him off the hook.

Chuckling, she shoved away from him, still holding the sheet to her chest. "God, your face! I'm kidding. Cash, honestly."

He blinked, held that confused expression a few moments longer and then gave her a very unsure half smile. "I knew that."

"I'm not the girl you left at Florida State," she told him. "I grew up, too, you know. I learned how the world worked. I experienced life beyond the bubble I lived in."

She took his hand and laced their fingers together. She still cared about him, so much. After that, she cared more than before. But she also wasn't so foolish to believe that sex—even earth-shattering sex—had the power to change the past. The past was him promising to wait for her and then leaving and never looking back.

"That was really fun," she continued. "I had a great time. You looked like you had a great time. I'm looking forward to doing it again if you're up to the task."

Don't miss what happens next in…
Second Chance Love Song
by Jessica Lemmon, the second book in the
Dynasties: Beaumont Bay series!

Available May 2021 wherever
Harlequin Desire books and ebooks are sold.

Harlequin.com

Get 4 **FREE REWARDS!**

We'll send you 2 FREE Books plus 2 FREE Mystery Gifts.

Harlequin Desire books transport you to the world of the American elite with juicy plot twists, delicious sensuality and intriguing scandal.

FREE Value Over $20

SPECIAL EXCERPT FROM

HQN

Here's a special sneak peek at
Follow Your Heart,
the fourth book in the Catalina Cove series from
New York Times *bestselling author Brenda Jackson.*

Coming soon from HQN Books!

Victoria knocked on the door to her great-grandmother's suite.

"Come in."

Opening the door, Victoria found her great-grandmother sitting in her favorite chair, knitting. Felicia Laverne Madaris had taught Victoria to knit when she'd been eight, and for her to still be able to use her hands to knit the way she did was amazing.

"Hello, Mama Laverne," Victoria said, leaning down to place a kiss on the older woman's cheek.

"And hello to you, Victoria."

Her great-grandmother was wearing a pretty floral dress with her signature pearls around her neck. Perched on her nose was a pair of reading glasses. While growing up, Victoria had thought her great-grandmother was one of the most stylish women she knew. She still thought so.

"You look pretty today, Mama Laverne."

"Thank you. And so do you. Would you like some Madaris tea?" Mama Laverne asked, placing her knitting aside and removing her reading glasses.

Victoria loved the Madaris tea. The recipe was known only to certain Madaris family members. "Yes. You want me to pour?" Victoria asked.

"That will be fine, dear."

After pouring them both cups of tea, Victoria noticed Mama Laverne studying her intently. She knew there was a reason for her doing so, and she figured if she was patient, her great-grandmother would tell her what was on her mind.

After taking a couple sips of tea, Mama Laverne said, "I'm sure you know why I wanted to meet with you."

Victoria nodded. "Yes, I do have a good idea."

Mama Laverne took another sip of tea. "I know some of you merely see me as a meddling old woman, intent on destroying your lives. But as you can see, I haven't steered anyone wrong yet."

Victoria chuckled. "No, you haven't. Nolan is happy with Ivy, Lee is happy with Carly, Reese is happy with Kenna, Luke is happy with Mac… Need I go on?"

Follow Your Heart *by Brenda Jackson*

HQNBooks.com